The Last
Crimes
of
Charles
Mistinguett

Novels *by* JAMES L. ROSS

The Last Crimes of Charles Mistinguett

Death in Budapest

Long Pig

The Last
Crimes
of
Charles
Mistinguett

a novel

James L. Ross

PERFECT CRIME BOOKS

Printed in the United States of America.
Perfect Crime Books™ is a registered Trademark.

This book is a work of fiction. The places, events and characters described herein are imaginary and are not intended to refer to actual places, institutions, or persons.

Library of Congress Cataloging-in-Publication Data
Ross, James L.
The Last Crimes of Charles Mistinguett / James L. Ross.
ISBN: 978-1-935797-46-3

First Edition: May 2013

For Mira

Long before I got to know Spain, I used to think
of Death as a Spaniard.   Arthur Koestler

1

I was abducted on Tuesday, the second evening of October, and became an accomplice to murder on Friday. French television has been merciless in hanging out my old laundry. They flash my picture every evening: a wanted man, dark complexion, surly mien (when that photograph was taken, the handcuffs hurt). They accuse Mistinguett the pied-noir, Mistinguett the extortionist, the pimp, the arsonist, the common thief.

The terrorist.

I have heard it all.

Once this is settled, I may emigrate.

On the Côte d'Azur, unhappy people seldom kill themselves in the high season. Even the discarded film star, considering a last fling with her pills, hesitates when the bright August heat might bring someone interesting to town. When the mistral blows its disappointing news down the hillsides, it is a different matter. October is a busy month for undertakers.

I was not ready to be undertaken. Contentment that has soured into boredom is seldom fatal. I had a table set out on the far edge of the Croisette, away from my hotel's customers. In the hills behind the town, villa lights shone, more inviting than the realities they decorated. The blue hour is a busy time. Madame Claudette, who had not done a film in nine years, would have summoned a young gardener for *amuse-pouche*. Monsieur Carl, the famed maître d', would be painting his toenails. Assorted Russian thugs would be talking to their stockbrokers in New York.

My blessings on all of them. Forty years ago, according to *Cahiers du cinéma*, Claudette's breasts were as important as bread. Monsieur Carl, when he comes to work in my restaurant, wears shoes. As for the Russians, they have other heads to break and leave mine alone.

"It is no wonder," my daughter said, "that Margaret despises you."

She sat across from me, sulky, full of grievances, young, irresistible. That morning, I had had her latest suitor run off, back to Italy. Until he had sneaked back, Suzy was desolate. I watched her while pretending to watch a yacht motoring out of the harbor. She was sixteen, moving away from me so quickly that I thought I had better steal a glimpse while I could. She resembled her mother in every respect, including a weakness for Italian louts, but I couldn't hold that against her. She said, "Margaret calls you a small, jealous man. Did you know that?"

"No." I didn't know she had said it. "Have you painted anything today?"

Margaret Aznavourian, my assistant who despised me, was teaching my daughter to paint. Modigliani was the girl's current god. Italian, of course.

"I'm painting myself nude. I'm going to hang it in the front window of your hotel."

"If you paint like Modigliani, no one will recognize you," I said. "There is Ali's ship."

My old friend's yacht was a half-mile out of the basin. Its rigging lights sprinkled a double Moorish arch across the sky, inviting anyone with hard currency to Kubla Khan's floating dome of iniquity. Ali exploited a popular belief that vice tastes better at sea.

My daughter ignored me.

The mistral was blowing. She was too young to notice.

She said, "Margaret cuckolds you every afternoon with a busboy."

I might have said, *That's one who isn't getting to you, pet.* But I knew better than to offer a challenge.

Instead, I patted the table. "Suze, go tell Margaret I disapprove of her having lovers. I want to sit and think."

She left, the cold wind picked up a little, and I was alone when Paul Chen—whom I had watched get out of a car along the Croisette—reached the table.

Even in the dusk, he wore the round little sunglasses of a pimp. His loose jacket billowed as he came past the tables. Rubber-soled shoes, pearl snaps on a white shirt, his short black hair blue in the fading light, if not a pimp then what? A record producer or hired muscle.

Across the street, there was a small crowd on the terrace of the Hotel Métropole. On this side, a dozen tables away from me, a waiter had delivered drinks to an elderly couple and gone. There were plenty of lighted shops along the busy street. Cars and motorbikes bleated past. The high season was over, and many of the faces at the playground had changed. But it was still Cannes. I was not truly isolated.

The car that had deposited Paul sat at the curb and waited.

He took the seat Suzy had vacated. "A man wants to see you."

Until a few years ago, he had worked for me. Now he served a Jordanian named Hamilton Hadad Adid, who rented motor scooters in Nice and—I had heard—used Paul to frighten shopkeepers out of weekly sous and pfennigs.

I said, "How is Hadad?"

"He has expanded, boss. Officially I work for Fintec, an insurance company. Number seven, Place des Moulins."

He seemed proud.

"In Monaco?" I said.

"By appointment to the Prince." He lifted a dark eyebrow. "Imagine the Prince appointing a crazed pervert to anything. Or going outside the royal family for a candidate."

I saw Jascha, who had come out of the hotel to wander along the promenade. Whatever her other faults, Suzy knew when to go for help. Puffing a cigar, trying to look like an adult, Jascha stopped and found something interesting to stare at on the beach while he waited to see what I wanted done.

When Paul worked for me, I had kept him away from the family. He didn't know about either Jascha or Suzy. Probably had thought, seeing her, that she was my mistress.

"Listen, this is a chance for you to make a friend," Paul said. "Hadad wants you to meet someone."

"I have enough friends."

"You have gobs of enemies."

"Still?"

He nodded. "You know, I've expanded, too, boss. Someone shot me."

Hadad sometimes lent out people to settle scores. But apart from my daughter, I couldn't think of anyone I had offended lately. It could be a joke. Hadad might have sent Paul Chen out with orders as vague as, Go down to Cannes, scare the shit out of Charlie.

Two men got out of the parked car and walked toward us, stopping a few feet from Jascha. They wore sweatpants and satiny hooded jackets. The short one held a knife. Jascha ignored him.

"Give me a hard time and the boy might get sliced up," Paul said. "Then we will put you in the car."

He overestimated his musclemen. Jascha was capable of dealing with the Neanderthals. But movie actresses aren't the only ones who dread the coming winter. I was fifty-six years old. Much less waited ahead of me than lay behind. How much less—who knew? I wasn't certain I wanted to make the journey to find out.

"It's an old man who wants to see you, a Spanish gentleman," Paul said. "He is harmless."

2

"The disappearance of Charles Mistinguett caused little distress among those close to him. No family member approached the authorities to report the abduction or to claim a body if one should be recovered. No mistress haunted the missing man's favorite beach wearing black. The daughter by his third wife summoned her Italian boyfriend back to Cannes. Several people who had entrusted money to Mistinguett were alarmed, but their concern was mainly that the business relationship might become public knowledge; the investments would be secure, for in his later years Mistinguett had become a conservative man. . . .

"A dozen policemen who had never been able to hang anything on Mistinguett pissed themselves with joy at the news of his death."

It is painful to know the contents of one's obituary. If Paul Chen dropped me in the sea, a gaudy warning that crazy Hadad was not to be offended, I might have enjoyed a brief epiphany. My life has been a waste, because . . . I wondered what it would be. Failure to join the priesthood? My mother's family had cast generations onto those empty waters. Anyway, my father would have disapproved. Then what? Failure to distinguish myself on a battlefield? There is little room in war for a prudent man.

We passed Pegomas, and the road twisted into the dark hills toward Grasse. The Neanderthals were both North African. Too stupid to be religious; Egyptians from far down the Nile. Paul had introduced them. The one on my left had a fat round face with protuberant eyes. He was called Munifal. The one who sat on my right had heavy knuckles, long shins, a jutting jaw. Gafar. They were silent. Paul Chen, who sat up front, hadn't told me the driver's name. I heard a few words from the man that marked him from Marseilles. While the brute drove, Paul carried on a cheerful phone conversation in some Asian dialect. Watching me in the mirror, he winked. I thought about asking if he had read Camus. Was there room in his brain to even consider absurdity?

We drove for almost an hour before turning onto a secondary road that two bends later became a lane. A wall on the left, an orchard on the right. Trees from both sides met overhead. We passed open gates and entered a courtyard. Part of the villa was low and dark, but in another wing lights glowed behind a screen of olive trees and I glimpsed a colonnaded room, swimming pool, indoor garden, people in evening clothes.

The car stopped. The lantern jaw opened the door, and I got out.

There were heavy smells of flowers, fruit trees, pines. A half-dozen cars were parked in a corner.

I heard the man before I saw him coming toward me. Each scraping step on the paving stones sounded like an ordeal. When he reached the blue light from the party room, it froze him for an instant: a figure of average height with white flesh and hair, clothing so dark it remained in the background. His hands trembled as they advanced a cane a half-dozen inches ahead of his step. I saw a narrow skull, lips sculptured by the underlying teeth. The least visible part of the face were the eyes, like spots of water hidden under the brow shelf.

Paul said, "Compliments of Monsieur Hadad."

The old man nodded. He presented a hand to me, and introduced himself in Castillian Spanish, "I am Carlos Gardel." The voice was harsh and dry. "Give me your arm. We will talk as we stroll."

When I didn't respond, he said, "I am counting on your curiosity making you want to speak with me. Of course, a younger man sometimes lets his feelings get in the way, especially if he has been offended?"

I gave him my arm, which he patted.

"My walking in the Montes de Leon was vigorous. Today a few steps tire me."

The Montes de Leon were the route of pilgrims in the Spanish Basque country. If he had been a pilgrim in that rugged and threatening terrain, it had been long ago. We minced toward a darker corner of the garden, his cane scraping.

"Hamilton Hadad does not know the reason for my interest in you," Gardel said, "only that I asked for his assistance. It's reckless, you know, to use one's own gangsters when others are available." The comment was meant to be a bon mot. His teeth showed briefly, like a ghost's. We came to a curved stone bench hidden near the path. Gardel nodded and wobbled in a half-circle. When his bony haunches were on the very edge of the stone, he released my arm.

"Not much matters to me," he said. "How can much matter? Next year this time, or perhaps the year after, I will be a bad memory, it is almost certain. Still, business goes on. I have a certain amount of money that needs a custodian. I couldn't come to you, in Cannes. Thank you for visiting me."

I said, "I run a hotel—"

We were totally out of the light. His voice was more intimate than I liked, as if we'd sneaked off in the dark to do indecent things. "I know, Monsieur Mistinguett, exactly what you do. You invest money of people who have been fortunate enough to accumulate a little. Your old associates, your friends, your ex-wives—though I suppose the wives' accumulations came from you, heh? Yes, I also know how you and several associates came by your money. You were criminals, m'sieu. No, no—I do not disapprove. A man does what he must. If I confided some of the things that I have done—oh, my! But we shan't discuss that. I will contribute a handsome sum to your capital. You may invest it as you have done for your other friends. My role will be that of a silent partner. You will find me no bother."

My father had died when he was relatively young, fifty-four, which had something to do with my sense that the time ahead for me was short. I had never known either *his* father or my mother's *père*. All my partners were more or less my own age. In short, I had had no intimate experience with a very old man, no point of reference when this one presented himself and expected to be treated as he demanded. If he had ambled into the Métropole with a bagful of cash, I might have offered him a drink and thrown him out.

I said, "I don't want your money, senor."

I felt him stir in the silence.

"We haven't established trust," he said.

"Do I have to call for a ride back to Cannes?"

"Monsieur Hadad's boys will take you home, when I say."

"Then perhaps—"

"Do you know Hadad well, m'sieu? He is a child of partition, the Palestine partition. His father was a Hashemite soldier in the Arab Legion, who so admired a British colonel—the colonel had hanged a Jew—that he named his son after him. Hamilton Hadad Adid. Political upheavals cast long shadows. The children of war absorb brutality by example. In Hadad's case, it doesn't help that the mind—the brain I should say—is organically defective. It imposes no check on the body's action. I worry about my having even a tentative association with him." He was silent for a few seconds. "But sometimes a man like that is necessary."

"Perhaps you could invest your money with him," I said.

"No, I would not do that."

"I would like to leave now."

"We have a few minutes. My servant offered Hadad's men a brandy."

"You seem to be having a party."

"I will return to my guests presently. As long as there is wine, they don't miss me. Let's discuss the matter of trust. It exists among you and your former associates because you know one another's history. How would we establish trust between the two of us? I thought about this before inviting you. The answer was obvious. We must become complicit in a crime."

The harsh old voice held no trace of humor.

"I asked myself, what sort of crime? Then I saw that this, too, was obvious. The crime must be murder."

I stood up. "Senor Gardel, you are mistaken about me. I'll call for a car."

"There is a prominent man who has caused me trouble," Gardel said. I heard less of his voice because I had begun moving away. A dry whisper followed me. "I will tell you his name and where he may be found. You will dispose of him."

I couldn't move quickly on the dark path, so I heard his next words.

"You have experience in these matters, have you not? I refer to Yves Bulant."

The name stopped me.

Yves Bulant.

I came back and stood over him in the cool darkness. The air had grown more fragrant, but rotten things often smell sweet. So do old men who crap their pants. Faint music throbbed in the distant wing of the villa. I thought of the beach across from my hotel. Mistral or not, the thought was fond. Even my daughter's temper was endearing. The old voice had faded to a scrape of crisp leaves. "If I had ever had a wife, I should certainly have shot her lover."

Yves Bulant.

Nobody in France faces the guillotine today. We're among the enlightened people who believe an axe murderer may be shown a new hobby. And for a crime of passion, a measure of tolerance is expected.

"Yves was not shot," I said.

He gave a soft hiss. "With Gardel, monsieur, it is all the same. Shooting, stabbing. However you wish it to be, it is."

"You've made a mistake. I don't kill people."

"However you wish it to be." The face was invisible. The dry voice whispered, "I hope you enjoy your ride back to Cannes."

3

Gardel was half right about Yves Bulant. My first wife had found him a dear. Where the Spaniard had learned the name I couldn't guess.

The Neanderthals let me off directly across the street from the Métropole. There were no police around, no camera trucks, no sign of alarm that a man had been abducted. I crossed the boulevard, climbed three steps. The lobby doors stood open. The two clerks at the reception desk scarcely noticed me. I walked to the back garden. We had a good dinner crowd, and Monsieur Carl the maître d' was having a drink at the table of a deputy mayor.

For some reason, the scenes of tranquility energized me. I took the stairs up four levels.

The door was open, and Jascha was waiting. "Your daughter is safe, patron," he said, answering a question he thought I should have asked. "And as you see, you needn't be concerned about me." He seemed to have enjoyed a meal in my suite. When I arrived, he was on the balcony, barefoot, impossibly handsome, cigar at his lips, admiring his image of himself. It was the image I had had of myself thirty years ago, except Jascha was taller.

"Was it a friendly meeting, boss?"

"Not at all," I said.

I sat down at my long, uncluttered desk. It occupied the middle of the room, with views of the bay from two balconies and of a massive cedar tree on the hotel's south grounds. Even this long past the season, the Croisette was ablaze with lights and busy with people. I had been happy in this room for years. Boredom had caused me to imagine I had stopped being happy. The suite was the largest and most luxuriously furnished in the hotel. Eight rooms, connected by short interior passages, provided accommodations for business, family and staff. The walls held no paintings of ancestors, but a couple of small landscapes could have covered the price of Gardel's villa. The desk on which I rested my elbows had belonged to Colbert's secretary.

"You gave no sign you wanted to be rescued," Jascha said. "I had Martino waiting with a car. He followed you."

"I noticed the headlights. You did well." It was I who had grown lax about security, reasoning that a man who has retired from the world faces no threat from it. Martino, our able-bodied gardener, couldn't have rescued me. But I hadn't wanted to be rescued.

I told Jascha, "Tomorrow we will begin a diligent search for a rat on board. Someone selling information."

Though nobody on the staff would have the story of Bulant to sell.

From a tactical standpoint, I was at a double disadvantage with Carlos Gardel. I knew nothing about him, and I had no idea whom he wanted killed. A prominent person with whom he had become displeased—a man, he had specified that much. The target's name had been unimportant to me at the time. Now I wanted to know more. Before going to bed I set a couple of inquiries in motion and came back in the morning to see where they had led.

Police agencies guard their information like old family recipes. By noon I had come up with nothing. The Interpol analyst in Lyon who had been intimate with my second wife found no reference in their archives to Carlos Gardel. I had left a message for the manager of a Santander bank where we had maintained an account. The manager, Inigo Lopez, responded that he could not vouch for the creditworthiness of Senor Carlos Gardel as neither the man nor his family was known to the bank.

I had already taken more direct steps. Martino and his grandson were mounting a round-the-clock vigil in a stand of pine a hundred meters south of Gardel's villa. He or Hugo would phone at every sign of movement. In six hours they had rung only once, when Hugo became excited at the arrival of a grocery truck. Several of the previous evening's guests had stayed overnight. Martino reported shortly after noon that two young women were making use of the pool. He knew there were guests, he replied tartly, because of the four vehicles parked at the villa only one had Cannes tags. Italy and Spain were represented. I cared nothing for who was visiting Gardel, unless a visitor's identity cast light on the host's. Martino read the numbers to me, and I wrote them down before he mentioned that all the vehicles appeared to be hired. I threw the note away.

My assistant Margaret Aznavourian attended to much of the rest of the morning's work. A well-run business needs little tinkering. It is easier to make one sound decision and to stand by it than to make a first decision and then—perhaps in the throes of boredom or a bad mood—reconsider and make a second, and so on. The first course had the merit of having attracted one in the first place. The second guess is seldom as good.

That morning nothing demanded more than passing attention. There had been a call from one of my partners, which Margaret described as routine. A prospectus had arrived from a company seeking to borrow additional money from our group. On first glance, Margaret approved. We set it aside. I finished biscuits and tea at eleven-thirty and found the desk empty. The morning was bright. My perfect assistant had gone off for a swim. My daughter hadn't escaped to Italy for a rendezvous with her boyfriend. Apart from the fact that Gardel had brought an ill-defined sense of jeopardy, life wasn't much different from the day before. A dull morning.

Not the kind to make one consider leaving the world.

There were more places I could ask about Carlos Gardel, but I had gone to the most likely sources first. Inigo Lopez knew something about any Spaniard whose wealth ran to nine figures; there seemed to be fewer of them every year. The fact he had never heard of Gardel meant my other sources probably hadn't.

Hamilton Hadad might have answers. He would be unlikely to share them.

He was, in fact, part of the question. Why would a man seeking an assassin look further than the thugs supplied by Hadad? There had been three right under Gardel's nose, four if you counted Paul.

Gardel wanted the job done with finesse?

I ate a late lunch with Jascha. He agreed it was idiotic that I hadn't made an effort to learn whom Gardel wanted murdered. "Suppose it was someone you also wanted removed, boss. A deal might have been struck." I stared at him, and he shrugged. "Not for us to do the deed. But a referral, perhaps?" It stunned me that he imagined I had a secret roster of murderers awaiting referrals. I wondered what thrillers he had been reading.

"It would be more productive," I said, "if you thought about how we could identify Gardel's target."

The challenge to his intelligence silenced him. He sat and thought, or pretended to think while he daydreamed. The table was on one of the small balconies, exposed to a perfect October afternoon, the summer hordes gone, the weather still warm, the light angular, the smell of the beach stronger than the traffic exhaust.

"It's possible," he said, "that the old man's only role is paymaster. Senor Gardel might have no personal connection to the victim."

"He claimed the man had displeased him."

"It might," the boy said, "be a really old grudge. Prehistoric. Untraceable."

Old man, old grudge—the link seemed facile. Jascha was watching a young woman on the sidewalk above the beach. His eyes were wistful. My demands left him little time for chasing girls. I declared lunch over and sent him off. For a while I sat brooding. It was my job to assess risk to Exports Méditerranée, Jascha's to mount a security program. Neither of us was doing a good job.

Margaret fetched her Lancia at seven, parked in front of the hotel, and was a few steps from the lobby when the bomb went off.

4

The only way to deal with intimidation is to make a show of getting on with life.

Our dinner at La Napoule had been scheduled since Sunday, when Jean-Marie Gassion announced he had arrived from Los Angeles. Margaret's Lancia was out of commission, so we took the SE down the coast with Jascha following closely in Martino's caravan. At Amortisseurs Jascha sat alone, separated from us by a half-dozen tables. The mistral pulled the tablecloth against my knees, and the shallow bay chopped the walls of Chateau de la Villeneuves, which surrendered its ruddy glow as the evening deepened. Tonight I had time to notice surroundings that otherwise were overfamiliar. Jean-Marie was late and Margaret had nothing on the agenda—nothing she wished to share; there is always something waiting for its moment. She sipped Lillet and flirted with someone two tables away.

I wondered how I could manage a few private moments with Jean-Marie. He was one of the very few people to whom the name Yves Bulant meant anything. And, Jascha's uninformed views notwithstanding, that was my obvious starting point—the fact Gardel had possessed the name to throw at me. It couldn't have come from Hamilton Hadad. Nor from Paul Chen. If there was an unseen hand behind Gardel, it was of someone who knew a great deal. I could almost tick off the names of those people on one hand.

The second wife, Edith . . .

Jean-Marie Gassion . . .

An old and dear friend, dead of natural causes . . .

Martino, just possible . . .

Elleston and Jonquil . . .

Suzy, no . . .

Margaret, certainly not . . .

Jascha, at his table, morose because she was looking elsewhere, knew nothing of those old days. His glory, for me, was of the here and now. This evening, though, he was displeased. I should never, *never* have permitted her to fetch the car, how could he maintain security when the patron was so lax, and so on, plunking the scorched bomb canister on my desk, voice rising, because had the attack been serious, *she* could have been blown to bits, and who then would manage Exports-Méditerranée, the complaint businesslike to cover his infatuation with the woman. Next time, he said ominously, with a twenty-year-old's certainty, it might not be all smoke and noise.

The fact that *I* might have stepped into a booby-trapped car and been blown to bits wasn't worthy of mention. He was also annoyed because I had refused to explain the incident to Margaret, had brushed it off as minor theatrics by Hadad. If she learned of Gardel's demand, she would dig deeper than Jascha had thought to do. She would ask, How could Gardel imagine such a thing of you, *mon cher*?

"Well, Charles! Margaret at least looks more beautiful each time." Jean-Marie Gassion looked at me from a round, cheerful, suntanned face that was accustomed to being disliked. There was a big scallop of bare scalp where hair had been, enclosed by short black fuzz that should have been gray by now. His garnet brown eyes had always suggested a good nature, tolerant of resistance. If the woman had not been present, I would have said something on the order of "Sit down, you treacherous bastard, and tell me the truth." As it was I looked pointedly at my watch, but he ignored the gesture.

He used a napkin on the chair. It's the sort of manners they teach in California. When he had ordered a kir, he tried entertaining Margaret with stories of Hollywood. She sipped her Lillet, played with the orange peel, listened with a charmed smile, and catalogued his shortcomings in a mental notebook that only she would ever read. At opportune moments, she pulled a line or two from the notebook and warned me about someone—never about Jean-Marie because she knew I understood him.

He had gotten a producer credit during the summer on an expensive comedy. No gimmicks, no mouse traps, he announced proudly—all due to hard work. He could get away with this guff with Margaret because I had never told her how he had "produced" films for the sex arcades in Germany. He was always gentle in dealing with the performers, who were prostitutes and drug addicts and needed harsh treatment to focus their attention. Jean-Marie cajoled, promised, procured and medicated his talent, and the process was time consuming and thus expensive. He did it that way so he looked better to himself than the industry's brutes. That was his moral yardstick: was some other person behaving worse?

The waiter brought huge trays of fried smelts. As Jean-Marie pinched a few, he said, "You know there is nothing like this in California?"

"No smelts?" Margaret said.

"But also no *this*." He waved a hand that took in the upstairs restaurant, the castle, a nearby marina, a dark and ancient sky. "There are wealthy people, beautiful ports, but L.A. at her heart is all slut—all commerce. The Côte d'Azur is about enjoying the fruits of commerce."

"Living off sluts?" Margaret said.

"The *spirit* of the place, dear."

It was all claptrap, of course. Commerce thrived along the Côte: the ports of Marseilles, Toulon, Cannes, Nice and Monaco all had their industrial faces.

"You, Charles," he said, "are all business. So I don't feel bad in asking how my investments are coming."

He had demanded a report ten days ago showing his account's value. The total was more than three times his contributions over the last half-dozen years.

"It seems to me," he said, "that we have not been setting the world on fire."

For the second time in less than twenty-four hours, I was shocked into silence. I dished around in my bourride, looking for something to punish. "Your rate of return is a little over twenty percent per annum," I said.

"Yes, I read the email. Dear Charles, I'm not complaining! Twenty percent is very respectable." He compounded his offenses by insisting he meant no harm. He poured the plonk I had ordered for him, raising his brows in inquiry. I could interpret that as I wished. Did I want my glass topped up? Or did I think there was more on his mind? "Of course, the partnership pays no dividend. So although the capital grows, for practical purposes it produces nothing."

Nothing, he meant, that he could clutch and spend.

Most of my investors preferred it that way. Their income from other sources satisfied their appetites.

"We could," I said, "pay you a small dividend."

"Certainly you could!"

I sipped the wine. It was obvious that Jean-Marie was strapped for cash. I try not to enjoy friends' embarrassment, but I was annoyed with him.

He pressed on. "If we're earning twenty percent, you can pay that amount."

"If we paid out our profits, we would forsake future growth."

Margaret gave me a look of disgust. She disapproves of cruelty, except sometimes. But I had had an unpleasant twenty-four hours—more than that, if you consider my frame of mind before Gardel's summons. And I couldn't think of a more likely source for Gardel's information than Jean-Marie. My troubles had begun two days after he arrived in France.

"Depleting our capital would be bad business," I said.

"Yes, yes, Charles, I see." He ducked his head, looking positively ill.

Margaret's lips parted. Whatever she had in mind—ridicule or sympathy—wouldn't be helpful. I sent her over to keep Jascha company.

After she left, I said, "What's this nonsense, Jean-Marie?"

"It isn't nonsense. Many partnerships pay a respectable return. I know several real estate companies right here—"

"They collect rents on their properties and distribute the income. That is not our business."

"The thing is, Charles—you've done very well for me. I'll be the first to say so. But I've been offered another opportunity. . . . "

"Ah."

"Perhaps safer."

I refused the bait. We had never suffered a setback of more than five percent. Nor were any of our businesses the sort that attract official interest. I said, "You would like to withdraw your capital."

"If it could be done."

"And all the talk about dividends was a pretext."

"I thought a dividend just might be possible and—"

"Do you need your money, Jean-Marie?"

"Regrettably."

"Your cinema work is not paying?"

"There are ridiculous expenses."

"And your other ventures?"

He struggled to remember how much he had told me. "The radio stations, you mean?"

I was silent. Margaret's interest in Jean-Marie's problems had not gone deep. She was laughing into her coffee and Jascha was looking pleased with himself. If one-tenth of the blockhead's attention was devoted to his patron's security, it was an invisible tenth.

I said, "If you wish your capital returned, it will be done. I don't regard the friends who invest with me as hostages." His look of relief vanished as I said, "But I think you owe me more candor than you've given."

He began his the-fool-misjudges-me routine, which I cut short. "You tried to convince me you were short of cash. In fact, you had convinced me. When I said it was a bad idea to deplete our capital, you turned green. I meant by paying dividends. Because you were hoping to close out your full investment, you worried I would be uncooperative about that as well."

"How long will it take," he said, "to get the money?"

"A few days, At the outside, a week."

"I'm not happy to desert you, Charles."

"You have this other opportunity. Of course. Call the office, and Margaret will tell you when we will have the check."

"Thank you."

"You realize there will be tax consequences for you? You have a substantial profit."

From his expression, it was obvious he had realized nothing of the sort, which told me how little consideration had gone into his decision.

I pretended cheerfulness. Our business done, I ordered brandy, not the best but respectable. I saw Margaret and Jascha follow my lead. Jascha lighted a cigar, man of the world, a little young, yes, but experienced, cultured, *puff*, perhaps he could convince her.

I looked back to my guest. "To your success."

"I wish there were another way," Jean-Marie said. For the first time I believed him. Taxes made a difference.

"Tell me about the new opportunity."

"A film," he said. "Several points are available in a film. It's very promising."

And less risky. He was a clumsy liar.

"What sort of film?" I wondered how much he had thought out, how much he could improvise.

"A costume drama, with religious overtones. Not your cup of tea, Charles. Mine either, but the public will love it."

It seemed to me the public's appetite for religious dramas had faded, if you didn't count the publics in Karachi and Tehran. But there was no film. I hadn't decided what *was* behind Jean-Marie's play-acting, but I knew that tonight he was telling only lies.

"As long," I said, "as your film is not about Yves . . ."

He frowned at his brandy.

" . . . I shall be happy. He would be a good subject for a film, dear Yves."

Jean-Marie's glance came up. "What are you talking about?"

"We are discussing the cinema and Yves Bulant."

"Cinema? You're discussing the dead."

"I don't think the artistic level would be high, do you? But it would be a story with commercial potential."

"You were always a sadist, Charles. It makes it easier for friends to turn away from you." He stared past me, at nothing. "I hadn't thought of Yves in years."

He left without finishing the brandy.

On the way home, Margaret said much the same things Jean-Marie had, I was a sadist, indifferent to the people close to me. If I was in trouble, she implied, it was of my own making. How she could imagine she knew this was beyond me.

"How will you redeem his investment?"

"I'll sell his interest to one of our other friends. I may buy part of it myself." I glanced at her, but she was silent. No mention of investing part of her own considerable savings in the business. There's a totally pragmatic side to Margaret. In her eyes I was never a low-risk venture.

While she drove, I phoned the surveillance post. Hugo was on duty. The villa's only new visitor had come and gone. It was my former employee, Paul Chen.

Alone?

Solo.

I wondered if Paul had gone to accept an assignment from Gardel that I had refused.

5

I sent Jascha up to Monaco in the morning to size up Fintec and look for signs of Hamilton Hadad's presence. Gaining residency in Monaco requires more than raw cash, more than decent family connections. It helps to have both, but the principality still may not want you. Doing business there is a bit easier.

I spent the morning reading newspapers, *Libération* and *Le Figaro*. Sometimes a mind gorged with ephemera chokes forth a useful idea. I sat on a balcony with my eyes closed to the sun. No idea sprang forth.

Margaret presented a draft valuation of Jean-Marie's account—far too high for the cement company. She went back to her computer and ten minutes later returned with Gassion's fortunes several hundred thousand Euros poorer. I called one of my silent partners, a retired civil servant, who was delighted to hear that shares were available at such an attractive price. He promised to wire the money before noon. He was my most complacent partner and deserved a bargain.

"Advise Gassion he may have a check tomorrow," I told Margaret. "Are there any fees we should deduct? Telephone calls? Postage?"

"I will deduct whatever you say," she answered, then went away.

There was an awkward moment in the afternoon when toughs from Gardel's villa took Martino into custody. Paul Chen relayed Gardel's demand: a case of the hotel's best Pauillac for the old fool's release. I sent a fifth growth and an hour later Martino telephoned, embarrassed. "They were using infrared devices, patron, and found us that way."

"They caught you in broad daylight."

"They had spotted us during the night, patron. Hugo was careless."

No doubt. Martino said he was fit to drive. To ease his embarrassment, I said I would devise a better surveillance method.

"They're having a good laugh," I told Jascha. "Gardel bombs my car, takes a hostage, accepts wine as ransom."

Jascha sat on the balcony, shirtless, drinking kir. "Still more than Martino is worth, patron."

"Gardel is an ass," I said.

Jascha was silent for a minute. "You know better, boss. You've made Margaret a virtual prisoner in the suites. She told me you forbade a trip to the hairdresser."

"I told her she could use the hotel's, which is perfectly good."

He snorted. "Your daughter is not speaking to you over a locking-in incident. You look at the hotel staff as if they might be traitors. You turn pale at the thought of Martino being injured. When I return from simple reconnoitering, you hug me like a school boy. I would say that Senor Gardel has brought considerable pressure to bear." I didn't protest, and he added, "At no cost to himself."

"Would you like to put a smoke bomb under his car?"

"I would like to put the senor in your position: waiting in trepidation to see what comes next. A real bomb? An employee returned dead? The game need not be one-sided."

He was eager for knuckle-busting—enthusiasm that would

have been useful in Ham Hadad's business, which relied on discipline. Unfortunately, I needed someone who could think.

"Tell me about Fintec," I said.

"The offices are where you said, Place des Moulins, number seven. Fintec occupies two small rooms in a six-floor building. It appears to be a company devoted to life and commercial insurance. Expensive rooms, patron, but I saw only two employees. There were no executives. A young woman who found me attractive said she didn't know the top people. Mostly this office performs data processing and financial management. There are sales and other operations in a number of cities, she said. If it were not for our security problem, she and I would be having dinner this evening." When I failed to commiserate, he went on. "There was no sign of Hadad, nor of his kind of people. The office was a good front."

"Did you check the rest of the building?"

"I hung around until I risked attracting attention. Hadad could have another suite, under another name. You wouldn't recognize Fintec as his if you just walked in the door. I know quite a few of Hadad's morons, and I didn't see any of them in the neighborhood."

"That doesn't prove anything."

He found his glass empty. Tossed it in the air and caught the stem.

"I could go up there and camp a few more days. But I think it's only an office."

"Then why would Paul have mentioned it? He told me Hamilton had a new company, Fintec, on Place des Moulins, and that it specialized in extortion, though he called it insurance. If he wanted to mislead me, he needn't have said anything."

"He may have told you all he knew. As I said, I didn't see any of Hadad's usual clowns in Monaco." Jascha considered. "I'm surprised he told you that much. Paul was being paid as a delivery boy. I don't talk to a bag of clothes I carry to the cleaners."

The answer was that Paul Chen still viewed me as a possible

employer. So he talked more than necessary, to impress me with his ambition. I was convinced Jascha had seen an important part of Fintec, whether or not it had registered on him. I had a different problem. Fintec didn't fit Hadad's personality. Data processing and financial controls? One might as well ask a cat to warble *Tosca*. Hamilton Hadad's version of selling insurance would be sending his monkeys out to smash the resistant grocer's windows. Consulting fees would be a few hundred Euros slipped to a *flic*. That was his level of sophistication.

Martino believed he owed me an opportunity to humiliate him. Instead of heading straight for the safety of his room behind the hotel, he came to the suite with Hugo lagging behind, head-bowed cap-in-hand sort of thing. The old man's sleeveless undershirt exposed bent hairless shoulders. His square face was downcast just enough that I couldn't see his eyes. His thumbs were hooked in his belt. If it were not for overwhelming forces and treacherous tactics, his stance said, Gardel's men would never have captured him. His grandson Hugo looked every direction but the old man's, embarrassed for them both.

Rehabilitation of my gardener-spy was in order. "So—how much did you learn, Martino? Were you in the villa?"

He had learned very little, it developed. Two armed men had driven him to the back of the villa and kept him in the kitchen while Paul Chen negotiated the ransom. The cook had been kind enough, giving him garlic bread and cold mutton. Martino had questioned the cook to little avail. The place was known as the Villa Balzar. The cook knew nothing he cared to tell about the present occupants. There were many armed men around the buildings, that was Martino's impression. But he had been isolated in the kitchen, so he couldn't be sure of anything. He hoped I understood. Trying not to stare at the red wine spots on his shirt, I said of course. In truth, I hadn't expected much from the surveillance. After a decent pretense at debriefing, I sent both men away.

A racket erupted somewhere near, and Suzy burst into the room followed by two of the housekeepers. She saw me and screamed. "How much of this do I have to take? I'm a *prisoner* in my room!"

"And a fine room it is," Jascha piped up.

"You're not a prisoner," I said.

"I can't go to Chat Noir!"

"Only for a day or two."

"But I *need* to shop."

Before Jascha could fan her flames, I said, "Then Jascha will take you."

His was horrified "Pop!"

I ignored him, ordered them out, followed the dispersing crowd as far as Margaret's office. I looked in. "When Jean-Marie calls, tell him we may have a problem with his money and he must speak to me."

I took the lift down, crossed the gardens, found Martino in his tiny room with a bottle of deep purple wine on the table. He poured me a glass. It was raw Provencal stuff that had collected in the bottom of a cistern.

I sat down. "Martino, did anyone else we know visit the villa?"

"No, patron. I told you about Paul."

"How long was he present?"

"Most of the day."

"Was he alone?"

"He arrived alone, in a gray Renault."

I described Jean-Marie. "Did you see a man like that?"

Martino rubbed his face. "Not on my watch. Do you want me to ask Hugo?"

"If you would."

He nodded, thinking that was that. I sipped the wine. We should have sent this poison to Gardel. "Martino, the old man up there knew a name from the past. Do you remember Yves Bulant?"

He'd have preferred to stare at the ceiling forever. But eventually he brought his gaze down and said, "No, patron."

"Of course you do. He was having an affair with my first

wife. You remember her, surely? Short, blond, good figure, a lisp?" Wet sibilants had come naturally to Mireille. Bulant had been infatuated.

"Ah, the blonde. What was her name?"

"Mireille."

"Mireille, yes, lovely child. Having an affair, you say." He didn't bother forcing a note of incredulity into any of that. "My Lil always stayed home."

"If you remember Mireille, you must remember Bulant."

His glance shied away. "No, patron."

"For God's sake!" I exploded. "It's all right to remember."

He coughed delicately behind his knuckles. "When one gets older, one forgets. Often it's for the best."

"No doubt." From Martino's reaction, it was obvious he believed I had murdered Bulant. No point in telling him the truth. If it had been in my nature to murder men who removed my wife's pants, I would have lined Montmartre with corpses during my last year with Genevieve. I said, "Whatever you think you know, old man, it is not the truth."

His expression turned quizzical—then almost hopeful—as he considered the possibility. But the belief had been with him too long. He looked away.

I had to ask the next question. "Have you heard that name mentioned?"

He shook his head. "Even now, patron, I have no memory of it."

I said, "Enjoy your wine, old friend." Given his suspicions, his loyalty was all the more touching. He would forgive my ancient crime and permit his grandson to work for me. Martino's Lil had been faithful, and I could be forgiven for not having been so lucky.

I walked through the garden. The evening business on the back terrace was comfortable, not too hectic for the waiters. I recognized several customers as long-term guests of the hotel. They may have recognized me as the same. Separated from the terrace by a line of apricot trees, I had no need to speak to anyone. A banker sat close to a woman of his own middle years whom I recognized as his wife, and for a moment I envied the stability of their bond without having any idea of its quality. Even a bad habit may be comfortable.

It's a revelatory moment when a young man finds his bride, to whom he has been faithful, in bed with another man. "In bed with" is a generic expression, more delicate than "riding astraddle on a rickety side chair." Revelatory, yes—about the bride, about one's loyal friend, about oneself. It wouldn't trouble me if memory said I had killed them both on the spot—a hard push against the chair back might have done the job. But nobody died on the spot, and then it was too late, as understanding seeped in. All love and passion depend on pretending not to understand, and once the illusion is broken there is no point being angry at the reality that shows through. I don't recall what Yves said as she scrambled off him. Time has manufactured a pleasant, "Why, Charles, who is minding the taxi?" He couldn't have had that much presence of mind. And I don't, in any case, recall answering at all about the taxi.

That is one of the problems any culpable person has—and any innocent one, too, in all likelihood. Memory lies. I wondered what Yves would remember.

Margaret was running down the hall as I came off the lift. Robbed of her composure, lightly flushed, she looked more alluring than usual. Among all the crimes attributed to me, sexual offenses so far have been overlooked. So I'll admit that a frightened woman stirs an atavistic response in me about equally erotic and protective.

She cried out. "Charles!"

The hall behind her was empty, and no looming peril filled it as the distance between us closed. My pulse slowed.

"Charles, it's Jean-Marie!"

"Here?"

"No, the telephone. He threatens to kill you!"

"I'm certain he doesn't mean it."

"When I told him his money was not available today—and

how could he expect it would be, you had never promised him that—he began screaming that he refused to be cheated by a *pied noir* and—and I'm afraid it got worse."

Her color was subsiding, and her breathing wasn't quite as rapid. (Who would deny the erotic aspect of this?) She walked briskly, half a step ahead of me. "I told him I wouldn't listen to garbage and he must speak to you." My sidelong look failed to make contact. "And he said how difficult it would be—for you— to speak to anyone because he was going to cut your throat."

He had spent too much time in Hollywood. If he cut my throat, he would never see his money.

The line was dead when I picked it up. I waved the handset at her. "He is on the way over to do the job."

"Why do you find that amusing?"

"Because so little else amuses me at the moment."

"And whose fault is that?" She paced in a fast circle around her desk. "You act as if your bad temper is my fault—or Jascha's—or the entire Côte's."

Hoping to head off a full-blown storm, I said, "No, I act as if there is a great deal on my mind."

"As if there isn't on mine."

"As if there is more on mine."

"It wasn't your car that received the bomb."

"A smoke cartridge. Yes, I know, it could have been Semtex. But that was not the idea, was it? The idea was to convince me Senor Gardel was serious."

"Senor Gardel? What about Hamilton?"

"I no longer believe he was responsible." I shrugged.

"So—Gardel. About what is he serious, Charles?"

"He would like me to kill someone for him."

"No!"

"He believes I'm capable."

She considered. "I've no doubt he's right, but for your own account, I think, not for a Monsieur Gardel's."

She too? I shook my head. I had never given her the slightest reason to believe it.

"Who is it?" She came around the desk, businesslike. Jean-Marie's silly threats brought panic. The possibility of my assassinating someone left her tight-lipped and practical. She and Jascha were soul mates. I described the meeting with Gardel, leaving out his trump card, and she said briskly, "You must talk to Gardel. However unpleasant you find him, you will learn something, won't you?"

The private line rang. I lifted the handset. "Yes?"

"Charles, my dear friend, I had to take another call." Jean-Marie spoke in a rush. "Margaret reports there might be a delay with my money." Tone friendly now, a sensible approach if another man has your money and you cannot open his throat to get it back.

"No delay, Jean-Marie, it merely takes time to raise the cash."

Silence. "Would you expect—"

"Soon. You have nothing to worry about."

"I'm certain—"

"Last night you said something I find curious. What did you mean about my friends turning against me?"

"I would never include myself."

"Of course not. But someone else?"

"I don't know, Charles. I was speaking in generalities. You had annoyed me, old friend, and I struck back."

"Would it annoy you again, Jean-Marie, if I tell you it may take several months—perhaps as much as a year—to liberate your capital?"

"Please, that is not funny."

"Unfortunately, the market in certain properties is depressed. An agent assures me we could not even find a bid right now for the cement company. As for our more liquid securities, I suppose they could be sold but the timing is awful; the shares markets in Paris and Geneva are depressed. And—"

"You bastard!"

"If business improves, all that could change."

"You treacherous African snake!"

"Don't be upset, Jean-Marie, the problem is only temporary. In a few months—"

His fury choked him. I set the receiver down on his curses.

"But you've already sold his interest," Margaret objected.

"So what? We'll hold Jean-Marie's money in trust for a little while."

She had never seen me betray a partner. But Jean-Marie, by his own choice, was no longer a partner.

"He may well try to kill you," she said in a tone implying he would be justified.

Jascha returned with Suzy. As the girl threw me a black stare and slunk away, Jascha remained. "She thought she could fool me. The Italian boy was waiting on a scooter. They were supposed to ride off together, but his scooter has become damaged. Also, you have a visitor downstairs."

That was quick. "Jean-Marie?"

"Paul Chen. Jonquil is entertaining him. Otherwise the coast is clear."

I ignored feminine nattering, sent its source to console Suzy, and took the lift down to have a talk with Paul.

"Are you here to kidnap me again?" I asked after I had brought a drink over to his table.

"No, but you should talk to the Spaniard again. He's not a man to mess with. I can tell you that first hand."

"You look to be in one piece."

He shrugged. "I know how to please a psycho. I got along with Hadad, you know?"

His hand bounced on the table, but there was no rhythm to it: he wasn't beating out a tune in his head.

"Fintec seems too sophisticated for Hadad," I said.

He nodded, but his attention wasn't there.

"Just personally, boss, if the senor wants something I would see that he gets it."

6

My second meeting with Carlos Gardel ended more disagreeably than the first. He laid out what he thought was a good table, with bottles from an expensive cellar, and waited for approval. The dinner was an offer of seduction if I didn't wish to be forced. But quail does not stand up to olive oil and garlic, and Cheval Blanc drunk ten years after its peak is just another aristocrat gone bad.

We sat behind the main house, on a balustraded terrace. Leashed dogs and their handlers prowled the outer grounds as if the Villa Balzar were a prison camp. Our small view took in a half acre or so of vines, heavy with fruit that should have been harvested in September. The vinegary fragrance of rot blowing across the flagstones largely masked the smell of the old man. How much of his stench was uremia, how much forgotten hygiene, I couldn't guess. It was a question to consider in twenty years, when my own olfactory nerves had gone numb.

He was formally dressed, playing the gentleman of a kinder age. The rest of his appearance made the claim a poor joke. There was nothing gentle in the bony face, nothing kindly in the deep-sunk and seldom-seen eyes. Every race is cruel, but Iberians have earned their special reputation. Only a Spanish priest could have dreamt up the Jesuits or their mission. Only a king from Aragon could have dealt so ruthlessly with the Moors who had civilized Granada. Gardel played at manners. Linen on the table. A gracious nod to his guest. But he ignored the convention that encourages occasional smiles in social settings. He neglected the rituals of small talk. Seduction was a nuisance if it was too demanding.

He also ignored the practice of encouraging loyalty among the staff. When a guard and his mastiff drew too near the balustrade, Gardel shooed them away like insects.

"You have had ample time to inquire about Gardel," the old man said. "The efforts will have produced little."

Less than little, but I saw no reason to say so.

"Curious," he said. "A man of apparent wealth, experience, pragmatism—yet unknown in the places one seeks help. What do you do if this man says you must kill someone?"

Torches yielded only feeble light and less warmth as the wind came down the valley. I wished I had worn a jacket over my sweater. Wished I had not come at all. Margaret was too optimistic about my learning something.

What do you do?

"I decline, as before," I said.

"Without knowing whom you are dealing with. But you have tried to learn, yes? And you failed."

"The most obvious answer," I said, "is that Carlos Gardel is a recently created name of convenience. So inquiries would be pointless."

If a bag of bones can pounce, he pounced. "Yes, that answer is obvious. The obvious is seldom correct."

"Another obvious answer comes to mind," I said. "It's that you fail to appear on official radar because you are too small."

His lips barely moved. "You know better. You were asking in the wrong places. You made assumptions about this old man Gardel and set out to confirm them. So—you inquired of the police? Perhaps international police—Interpol? And they checked their files and found no trace of Gardel. Where else did you inquire?"

I wondered if he was merely guessing about my call to Lyon. In any case, I had no intention of giving him clues that could lead to Inigo Lopez. I said, "I have excellent contacts in Paris."

"Who found nothing. Gardel is not listed anywhere under 'Criminal.' You would be amused if you knew my previous career."

There was something about the arrogance. It was arrogance I had encountered before. He would not have been seen as wealthy during his career, because he would not have dared. That let my Santander banker out. He wouldn't have been known as a criminal. That kept him out of the files at Lyon. But he was an expert on crime.

Normally I can pick them out of crowds, but he was very old, long retired.

"You were a police official," I said. "Or a prosecutor. Something that fed your natural vanity."

He was silent for a few seconds.

"A policeman," I repeated.

He finally spoke. "That is very clever of you. Now you must tell me how you know."

"I don't. You could have been a soldier. Or a diplomat. Your bearing is official. It stands out." So did a streak of sadism. And contempt for everything that fell across his gaze.

He made a dry laughing sound. "No, you found a source. You will tell me later. It will be part of the sealing of the bond between us." He leaned forward, and the torchlight reached the eyes. They looked like jellied eggs. "What interested me most in most in my days wearing a uniform were fragments—something between rumor and fact, depending on what one sought in them."

He stretched out a trembling hand, as if I had been about to leave. "Do you understand? Knowing a little about Yves Bulant, I know everything about Charles Mistinguett."

"Assuming you know anything," I said.

"I've had many years knowing things. Fragments—bits and pieces. I am like a collector of old metal buttons. A new piece surfaces. One wonders at the unfamiliar design. Was this from a military jacket? If there is a cross, does it signify a religious order—or has someone appropriated the symbol of the Savior to worldly ends? A man must collect diligently. A year after the first, a second example appears. Then more quickly a third, because the eye has been alerted. Then—what have we?"

"Enough for a suit coat," I said.

"No, an insight into something that may have existed right under one's nose. Now one begins to see things as they truly are."

People in France who talk this way—looking for patterns in ephemera—tend to imagine the Masons are secretly pulling society's strings. At least . . . I assumed he didn't mean, literally, buttons. He meant fragments, which could be sorted and arranged, if one had patience. The picture they formed might show the Pope wearing devil horns or Kabbalah written on the Élysée curtains.

Gardel wasn't a Frenchman. He might not care about Masons or Jewish plotters. If anything remained of the disciplined cop's mind, he could be formidable. Or he could be batty.

I toyed with my wine glass. "So you are a policeman looking for patterns."

"Retired, retired. A normal policeman could not afford this villa. For me it is pocket change."

"Thanks to your fragments."

"Now I will tell you what I observed that pertains to you. There is a social aristocracy in France, as well as much of Europe, that operates in what is called—inexplicably—the public sector and does very well for itself."

He stopped, expecting a response. I accommodated. "How many years of button-collecting did it take you to notice this?"

"Oh, yes, everyone is aware of Europe's political class. Its self-serving habits also are well-known. The larger and more powerful our bureaucracy grows, like a great feeding pen, the more the political class fattens itself." His mind seemed to drift. "It astonishes me that there are not more revolutions. A lurch to the guillotine—who could object on moral grounds?"

"Assuming your revolutionaries knew whom to guillotine."

"They would charge in the direction their new masters pointed them. Never suspecting that the game has been repeated a thousand times through history. A string of scandals—the defense minister's secret avionics investment, the justice minister's criminal dalliances, the president's bank accounts— stirs public anger. A flamboyant opportunist rides in on the white horse of virtue. The rabble are told they must have blood for justice, so they demand it." When he leaned away from the table, the eyes and cheeks sank out of sight and the bony face had a corpselike stillness. He was old enough, he could have died just like that. I waited and heard him breathing.

"The scandals you mention were reported in *Le Monde*," I said. "Nobody hopes for white horses, except for a few lamebrains in the National Front, and nobody expects virtue. The average Paris taxi driver is as cynical as you, Senor Gardel, and as well-informed. He contents himself voting Communist knowing they won't win."

"You are impertinent."

"No offense intended." But it had been. On my first visit he had been all snickers and smirks. Tonight his dignity was brittle. He had been miffed by my refusal to kill for him. Now I had deepened the insult by refusing to appreciate the broad picture he wanted to paint: a corrupt Europe, its masses seething, primed for turmoil. At that moment, I thought he was insane, but no less dangerous for it. Later, when I learned something of his early politics, I understood the fantasy's resonance for Carlos Gardel.

"You are also complacent," he said. "Humanity will not deny itself justice forever."

I drank the dead wine.

"I would not want you to believe I care about humanity or justice," he said.

"Of course."

"But the extreme degree of official criminality intrigues me. You argue that the common man is so morally lethargic that nothing will be done. Perhaps I should concede the point. 'Someone will steal,' the worker tells himself, 'and Gaston or Herbert at least promises me a thirty-hour week.' What are a few hundred billion siphoned Euros if this dolt gets to sleep late? I care nothing of that anyway. No, my interest is your role. You are outside the political class, but you are indispensable to them."

"How is that?"

"No, Monsieur Mistinguett! You will not conceal yourself behind puzzled smiles this evening." The invisible mouth crunched its dry sticks. He spoke with quiet vehemence. "You will not pretend to think I am senile. You see, I know a great deal about you. I know that you are a competent man in your field. That field is handling money for people who must remain in the background. They remain hidden, Mistinguett, because their money is soiled. You serve the criminals of the political class."

Fewer than a third of my business partners had ever held jobs of public trust. But I didn't say this. I didn't want to give the old man even negative information.

"You do not appreciate honesty," Gardel said.

"I don't appreciate threats."

"They are part of a businessman's life. We shall do business. You will find it too dangerous to deny Gardel."

"I would find it more dangerous to kill someone."

"I can speak personally: ending a life is not difficult. As a moralist, I can speak as well: how many men truly are worthy of existence?"

I didn't answer.

"The worst fallacy is sentimentality. We recognize a man as an obstacle but hesitate to act because he is a child of God. The evidence of such parentage may be elusive, but still the sentimentalist hesitates. A human life"—he coughed softly— "mustn't be sacrificed, except in a time of war, or in a period of ecclesiastical upheaval. Then we are expected to be bloodthirsty. But never for one's own convenience."

He expected me to admire those pearls. I said, "Who is your target?"

"I have approached a man on a reasonable basis—my discretion and assistance were offered, at a very modest fee. He has refused me out of hand. His name is General André Guiot."

I had never heard of him. "French?"

"Yes."

"Why assassination?"

"It will help me believe that you and I can cooperate—perhaps even collaborate. I find your business attractive. It has low capital requirements, large returns, and many ancillary opportunities. For example. How many of your corrupt clients would be in a position to complain publicly if you changed your fee structure to their disadvantage? How many could remove their capital, and explain its existence to the tax authorities? A man in a business such as yours—and mine—holds a much stronger position than you realize."

"If you're already in the business, you don't need me."

"That was Monsieur Hadad's view. If I had him as a partner, for what would I need you? He saw no value in subtlety."

He had barely touched the quail or the wine. A heavy man in a black jacket brought a tray of flan and coffee.

"I hope you appreciate my kindness regarding your spy," the old man said. "It was only because we had not established guidelines. Now we shall. You must not send watchers again. Nor should you attempt a more covert kind of surveillance. I would find out, and there would be reprisals. Don't bristle. These are not threats. You are being given guidelines. A common failing of the criminal is an abhorrence of discipline. This is not, I realize, one of your shortcomings. But you have been used to your own discipline, now you must adjust to mine. You must look beyond your own demanding judgment, and consider a layer of judgment above your own." The voice was devoid of passion and the sense of things to lose. It was more convincing than Jean-Marie's screaming anger.

"If you think you're under surveillance," I said, "please ask me."

"No. If I think I am under surveillance, I shall act. Don't object. I know, you will say I might be mistaken or the watchers might be working for someone else. I consider that irrelevant. I haven't time to negotiate with you along each step of our merger"—that was taking it further; he had said cooperation or collaboration before—"so you must learn quickly. If I act and the surveillance continues, I will know you were innocent. But that will do no good for Mademoiselle Aznavourian. I thought my demonstration was adequate. A young woman is vulnerable in more places than you can count. If I had intended to harm either of you, there were many opportunities last evening—the automobile, Amortisseurs, the highway. You were never alone. Would you like to know mademoiselle's dinner?"

I wouldn't. My stomach had lost its bottom. An old spider would be the most dangerous, its poison concentrated.

"Excellent. I am very tired now. Paul will see you home. On the matter of General Guiot, Paul will assist you. It will be excellent advertising for our services, a demonstration that we are serious. Paul must make one stop. You won't begrudge him a few minutes, as he acts at my behest."

As he sank back, a finger rose into the light like a pale bone. "You should eat your flan, m'sieu."

We were a few miles above the coast when Paul Chen stopped the car and popped open the trunk. The third passenger in the car had ridden in the trunk in silence.

7

There was much to think about, none of it pleasant. I had no intention of collaborating with Paul Chen on an assassination. During the last ten minutes of the drive, I concocted bloody finales for both Paul and Gardel. The daydreaming neglected the fact I was no good at that sort of thing. If I had been better at violence, I might have approved of it more. Exploding vehicles and long-bladed knives might be instruments of justice, but it was a justice I was incapable of delivering.

Yes, I know. My reputation as a cutthroat has been established—largely through lurid accounts by the kind of television programs that pay gardeners to photograph sunbathing celebrities. But I wish to put my innocence on the record.

My first practical thought, as we came down toward the coast, was to send Margaret away. But doing so wouldn't give me freedom of action. She wasn't, as Jascha would remind me, my only point of vulnerability.

Besides, she was too valuable an ally.

As Paul drove, he had described jobs for Hadad. In the years since I had sent Paul out to flim-flam bankers, he had roughened his skills. He thought the newer talents were more manly. In Nice he had strangled a man with a bicycle chain.

"Is that when you were shot?"

"Yeah." He drove for a couple of minutes. "Stupid. The job didn't help Fintec, it just made the pervert feel good."

He had stopped the car on the mountain road.

We unloaded Hamilton Hadad's corpse from the trunk to the roadside, where it would be found.

"Paul Chen—new chop boy," Paul said, as if introducing himself, and bowed. "The Spaniard has asked me to work for him." His round face quivered. Having seen men on the verge of self-discovery before, I recognized Paul's mix of anticipation and horror. Breaking elbows wasn't enough. A new man was emerging. If Gardel knew what Paul had done to Hadad, he must also know that his new chop boy was going to be hard to control. But perhaps Gardel had ordered it that way: messy and impressive. I have never suspected policemen of having subtle minds.

For the rest of the drive, Paul was chatty. Mostly he warned me against underestimating the Spaniard. He was a pervert, like Hadad, but swung to a different beat. "Control, total control. Those girls he keeps up there, he doesn't touch them, but he tells them what to do, when to have breakfast, when to go to the bathroom. We had lunch today, four of us, and it was like watching one of the dolls my sister had. You pull a string on the back and it talks. I'll tell you, it was scary."

"What does he want with Fintec?"

"Extortion. Ham had eight, nine people he called clients that he was squeezing. Some of them were people he had bribed. He said a bribe was only a temporary expenditure, it came back with interest. The old man wants to own a lot of things. Including you. So. If you had to kill a retired general who lives in Maisons-Laffitte, how would you do it?"

"Send a retired policeman."

"Ha! You're still funny. But he's an old shit on a cane, so we have to do it."

"I'll have to think."

I felt better after a change of clothes and a shower. Before bed I told Margaret to leave a message for Jean-Marie that we would have his money after all, tomorrow at noon. Would he please stop by.

Making love proved impossible. In place of Margaret, I saw Hamilton's excorporated head and scornful eyes. It had ridden with us in a separate canvas bag. In the end, I felt myself tumbling after the head into a ditch. The sensation of having become detached from my body was quite vivid.

I got out of bed, returned to the office. It was three in the morning. I summoned Jascha.

The boy's recommendations on security were short-sighted. He crossed the bare feet resting on my desk. "Get Gardel, patron. Right now. Before he gets you."

"I think we can take reasonable precautions."

He held his hands wide, then clapped them together. The air rang. "That was a rocket fired from the street through the window behind you. What 'reasonable precautions' would have saved you?"

I was silent.

"Gardel is a terrorist. He can strike when he wishes."

"I was thinking Suzy could take a vacation," I said. "You could keep an eye on her."

He snorted. "I am not a baby sitter, boss. But then what? Would you never see her again? This man may have a long memory."

I almost said he wouldn't live forever, but how old did I make him? Late eighties, early nineties? He might live five years, poison sacs intact.

"There are options besides killing the man," I said.

Jascha rolled his eyes at the ceiling.

"That's Gardel's brainless tactic," I insisted. "A man is difficult, drop him in the sea! Gardel's system and Hadad's."

"Both of whom would tell you it is effective." When I didn't argue, he went on. "You're dealing with a *flic*, remember. The old pisser wants a hold on you."

"It seems he's found several."

"No, he can't be sure. He doesn't know if you are sentimental. If he were on the spot, he might consider a mistress or daughter expendable. Not that he would give them up easily, but a threat to them wouldn't decisively tip the balance." He stared at his toes, wondering if he wanted to deliver his next observation. "May I point out, patron, that a threat hasn't tipped the balance with you? You are still thinking resistance. So Gardel has thought ahead. If there were photographs of you shooting a general, you might behave."

I sent him back to bed. He had said nothing I hadn't already considered.

Of course Gardel wanted me under tight control. He must have learned a lesson with Hadad.

And if they merely wanted Guiot eliminated, Paul Chen had proven himself up to the job.

The question wasn't why Gardel wanted what he wanted — but how I could avoid giving it to him.

I wondered if Hadad had thought that way. He couldn't have taken kindly to a retired cop moving in on his business. I should have asked Paul how long there had been any affiliation between the two. The answer might have told me how fast Gardel moved.

Aznavourian was businesslike that morning, neither disgustingly cheerful nor evasive. I had not offered a reason for my failure. Perhaps she imagined I had lost interest.

She reached Jean-Marie. I found lowly situated friends in the Basque provinces who recognized the name Gardel. Nothing they said made me feel better. "The Carlos Gardel I recall was never a regular police officer," said Miguel. "The monster I remember was a security officer, of the *policia secreta*. He made a name for himself in the Civil War. If he is alive, he is very old. This man will be in his nineties."

"That sounds right," I said.

"He must be very feeble."

"In some respects."

"He told you he was with the police?"

"No, he let me believe it."

"Perhaps he thinks of himself in those terms. What difference does the insignia make?"

"Tell me what you know," I said.

"Yes, yes." During the war, he wanted me to understand, the Republicans were far from unified. Fighting more or less on the same side were elements from trade unions, anarchists, Trotskyists, Stalinists, Catalan and Basque regionalists—all enemies of the Carlists and Falangists but also distracted much of the time fighting among themselves. The purity of truth was never more important than in the nineteen thirties, did I understand? Alliances of necessity were temporary. In thirty-six, seventeen-year-old Carlos Gardel was one of Stalin's executioners, thinning the ranks of anarchists in Barcelona. In thirty-seven, he switched sides from the Republicans to Franco.

"Have you heard of Durruti?" I hadn't, of course. Miguel explained. Early in the war, Republican volunteers at the front took women with them; in fact, every ambulatory prostitute in the region swarmed the undisciplined camps. Thanks to these *milicianas*, syphilis spread among the Republican forces faster than dysentery, and casualties from knife fights over women rivaled those inflicted by Franco's bullets. Durruti saw disaster looming. There were no officers as such—Republican idealism and so on—and the fighting spirit was waning. The men refused to advance unless the women advanced as well. So Durruti concocted a story of a "rest and recreation" center, to which he would first transport the whores, and then the deserving soldiers for a long leave. Trucks were summoned. Scores of women boarded. Some miles from the front, the trucks stopped. The women were unloaded, and security troops machine-gunned them. Durruti was a simple believer in revolution, not adept at sinister twists. His security officer was a young Basque who believed in nothing. Would Charles wish to guess the Basque's name?

I wished. "Carlos Gardel."

"Very good. You see how Gardel could transfer his services. He was too valuable to execute."

After the war, Captain Gardel was ruthless in his persecution of former Republicans. It wasn't the passion of the convert that drove him. Republicans happened to be the people who, at that time, could legally be tortured. "He wouldn't have minded priests," Miguel said. "He hated priests. He hated jurists. He was antipathetic to the idea of any sort of justice. Convenient for a secret policeman, no?"

"He could dispense his own justice," I suggested.

"No, no, you idiot! He could dispense *whatever he pleased*. And he would be immune, because justice is an illusion."

"He implied to me that he had made the Pilgrimage."

It is a profound matter for many Spaniards, the Christian's trek to Santiago de Compostela.

"*Ambulare pro Deo*? To wander for God? It just shows you, Charles. Not everyone wandering in the mountains is a pilgrim."

Miguel went to his restaurant and I sat at my desk and thought about the old man. I've no sympathy for amateur psychology. What a Frenchman shrugs at, others analyze— always foolishly. But there was something about Gardel I needed to understand. I had glimpsed his nihilism the first evening and thought it was the indifference of age. Now I had been told nihilism had been with him for seventy-some years. What age had brought was freedom. Today Captain Gardel could torture whomever he pleased.

I kept the inquiries distant, made no attempt to learn whether he owned or leased the villa, didn't look for local bank accounts, and decided—as Fintec was now Gardel's— that he might take a second investigation by Jascha as "surveillance."

I asked Margaret to prowl reference sources for any information on General André Guiot, regiment and age unknown. She could follow any leads with discreet telephone inquiries. If Gardel got word of my interest, he could hardly object. I was checking target and terrain—basics, for assassins.

My old friend Jean-Marie arrived well before noon. He was transparently suspicious that I would change my mind again. We had lunch on the hotel's front terrace, very much in the open, business as usual; having accepted Carlos Gardel's mastery, I had no reason to fear him.

"Margaret will join us when she has the check," I said. "Unless you would prefer a bank wire?"

"A check is acceptable," he said stiffly. It took me a few minutes, a dozen early oysters, and a good bottle of Muscadet to soften him up. Lies also helped: I explained the lengths I had gone to creating liquidity in our partnership for his sake. I elaborated on how grateful I was for our long friendship. Told him that if I had seemed distant these last few days, it was from personal pressures. That lifted his eyebrows.

"Margaret?"

"No. She still tolerates me."

"Ah." Disappointment thinly disguised. To pick up a large check and a woman in one visit was well within his expectations. In California, even an unattractive package such as Jean-Marie might have found that possible. In Cannes, the check would need to be larger. He said, "The children, then. You remind me of why I remain a happy bachelor. If there are little Gassions, they wear some other gullible clod's name."

"No," I said with a sigh. "Suzy has a dago suitor, but otherwise I've no reason to complain."

"Ah."

I stared blankly at his shoulder. His choices were limited. He could change the subject, or he could pretend diligence. A person with something to hide would press on.

"What then?" he said.

"In all truth, Jean-Marie, it is business. But I know you've heard or you wouldn't be withdrawing capital."

The tanned face struggled. Should he appear surprised?

I prodded: "What exactly have you heard?"

"Well . . ."

"Well?"

"I had not heard, Charles, that there were business problems."

"What then?"

"Hmm."

"What?"

"There is a rumor that Hamilton whatshisname is making war on you."

"So what?"

"The suggestion was made that it could be dangerous to remain on your team." Having leaned toward me as his voice dropped, he jerked back. Being physically close could get one mistaken for the wrong team.

I felt contempt for Gardel's tactics. What was I supposed to think? That he could frighten off a rabbit?

I wondered how the old man had learned Jean-Marie's identity.

"I'm disappointed in you," I said. "Why didn't you tell me about this?"

"It was obvious you knew. You don't usually arrive at dinner like a mafiosi with his bodyguard. I was startled you exposed Margaret to the danger."

"You didn't know how I would arrive at dinner. We spoke by phone before that and you said nothing."

"Well . . ."

It took fifteen minutes to get the details. Two brutal-looking Egyptians had visited his hotel. They said it would be looked on favorably if he ended our relationship. Very traumatic for Jean-Marie, who had never encountered thugs in Hollywood.

"What about Yves Bulant?" I asked.

Jean-Marie shook his head.

"They didn't have that name until you gave it to them," I said. "Did they?"

He mumbled something.

I don't make many mistakes, but I take full responsibility for the blunder I committed then, and for the misunderstandings that flowed from it. If Jean-Marie had showed even a dull sliver of courage, I wouldn't have been so tempted to terrorize him further. I said: "You're welcome to take your money and make your movie, or spend it however you wish. Margaret is just inside with your check. But you should not run away because of Hamilton Hadad Adid. He is waiting to be noticed along the N85. Though identification may require patience."

In our youth Jean-Marie and I had broken many laws together—most of them absurd attempts by the Republic to regulate commerce. But we had relied on our small stores of cunning over force. He looked at me with the awe I had tried to conceal as Paul Chen described himself as a chop boy. Sort of: Oh, so you've gotten the knack of doing that, have you?

And he understood that what I could do to Hadad, I could do to a disloyal friend. He squeezed himself tight to hold in a question: Why would identification take patience?

Margaret timed her arrival perfectly. She stood a large gray envelope against the Volvic bottle, within Jean-Marie's easy reach. His hand controlled itself.

I said quickly, "Mademoiselle Aznavourian does not know much of what I've told you."

His look was as good as saying he wasn't surprised. He swallowed hard. "We'll talk of more cheerful things, then," he murmured. "My cinema projects. You should consider investing, Charles."

I shrugged. He chatted nervously about films, about politics—the mayor of Nice had been indicted—about the pathetic French economy. Neither I nor Margaret did much to encourage him. When lunch was over, I had to remind Jean-Marie to take his envelope. It was a moment of truth. He made a simpering gesture. "Really, Charles."

Had thought of reasons a body could be hard to identify.

"I insist," I said. It came out harsher than I had intended. I softened the rest. "Give yourself twenty-four hours, old friend. Then if you are comfortable remaining in the partnership, you may destroy the check. Otherwise—"

"There is no need. I am comfortable."

"But I want you to be certain." I wanted any observer to see him departing with an envelope. Better if Gardel believed his attack had done damage.

When Jean-Marie was gone, Margaret said, "What haven't you told me?"

"Only unpleasant details. We're still at risk. He doesn't know that."

"You deceived him."

"True."

"What happens if he chooses to remain in the partnership? You have already sold his shares."

"I will find a way to invest his money. Several companies would welcome the capital." The waiters at the Métropole know better than to present bills to my table. The hovering of our waiter became noticeable. When I stared at him he came over, an older Italian they called ZiZi. He asked loudly if there would be anything else and added almost inaudibly that we were being watched from Antonio's section.

"Another bottle of water. Which table?"

"The couple. He with the beard."

He returned with the water in a minute but had nothing more to say.

I filled both glasses. "Tell me what you've learned about General Guiot."

"Wealthy, political—a typical general, or what they would like to be. He is what they call a peacetime general." She had no notes. "He was never in combat and never commanded men in combat. That is quite an accomplishment when you think of the opportunities in the last forty years."

"How old?"

"Seventy. He became a general when he was very young."

"But he is retired?"

"He is not on active duty."

"And?"

There was more—career, family, politics, business connections. The general had written books on battlefield tactics. He was a faithful husband to a childless wife. He was a neo-Gaullist. He was a director of a steel company and a bank. A man of substance. As long as she had a computer and a telephone, Margaret was infallible. But I couldn't resist challenging her.

"The noncombatant wrote on battlefield tactics?"

"The books describe computer-generated battles involving the use of nuclear weapons. You see? The general's expertise hasn't been field-tested. And who is the person watching us?"

I had spotted the couple long before ZiZi noticed their interest in us. The woman was less than nondescript, in fact homely, a *hausfrau* on holiday. The bearded man was too good-looking to be her husband or lover. They were colleagues.

"*Flics*," I told Margaret, "no doubt looking for crime in the soup."

"Both of them?"

"I recognize the man—Laval, don't know the rank; he arrested Paul once."

"For what?"

I shrugged. I remembered perfectly. Murder. Paul had been innocent that time.

"What do we do?"

"Ignore them."

"There might be a listening device."

"Laval wouldn't be seen in that case."

"What can he want?"

"A lunch on the taxpayer, my dear. Would you like a swim this afternoon?"

"We're not on holiday."

"That could change, and a change might be in order." If Ali

Souidan invited us for a cruise, we would be beyond the reach of Gardel, his chop boy and the French police—long enough that some of the dangers might cancel each other. How would Laval respond to a message that Paul Chen had murdered someone for real this time?

We went upstairs. Margaret and Jascha swept the rooms for bugs. There is no such thing as true security. We satisfied ourselves that nothing unsophisticated was in use. If there were state-of-the-art devices, we could do nothing.

I placed a telephone call to my lawyer. He was taking his typically expansive lunch hour, so I left a message. An old problem had reasserted itself. Could we discuss it?

I had barely set the phone down when Paul Chen called. "Our patron is getting itchy," he said.

8

I spent the afternoon trying out solutions that didn't involve murdering Gardel. The most obvious was to denounce both Paul and the Spaniard to the police. But that would be effective only if the authorities moved quickly and efficiently. The idea was so feeble that if Jascha had offered it I would have batted him on the head.

On the few facts I could provide, the police might not move at all. They would be a dangerous ally, in any case. They might prefer to listen to Gardel make accusations against me.

By late afternoon, my mental effort had produced exactly no improvement on Jascha's recommendation.

Perhaps I could settle for partial solutions. The immediate problem was Gardel's plan for General Guiot. I felt no obligation to preserve the general's skin—at least that was not a very high priority. People die in Paris every day, in every city, every hamlet, yet few of us devote much energy to resuscitating strangers or lecturing them on safe living. I don't mean to be callous, but I had only the thinnest knowledge of André Guiot. The possibility that he deserved to die many times over wasn't lost on me. My sole objective was not to participate in his murder. That and not confront Gardel.

It bothered me how little I had understood Paul Chen. When he worked for me, especially in the first year, I had looked on him not only as an assistant but potentially as a protégé. He had gotten a rough-edged education in Malaysia and Hong Kong and understood bankers, if not banking. Since my capital was still insignificant, we had to focus on the men rather than the institutions. Paul's instinct for exploitable weakness was nearly infallible, perhaps because it wasn't obscured by a normal sense of mercy.

The currency of bribery is varied. Margaret initially worked with me in that capacity. We called it cultivating clients. She slept with few of them. When it became obvious that this twenty-four-year-old from a decadent family had a good mind, I promoted her to more demanding duties. She claimed never to have resented my early stupidity. I saved her, she says, from a life of bored mediocrity. That's nonsense, of course. She could never have been mediocre, though I suppose she might have let herself become bored.

Paul's career went the other way. He was as good as he seemed at the start—cruel and clever—but he never developed more refined skills. His grasp of banking remained superficial, which limited his usefulness. When I sent him back to Hong Kong carrying a letter of credit on a Geneva bank, a suspicious shipper's agent had him arrested within forty-eight hours. Even when the bank vouched for the letter, it took two months and tens of thousands of francs in legal expenses to get him released. The Crown prosecutor knew a swindle was afoot but couldn't spot the target. Neither, fortunately, could the Swiss bank, which had written the letter against dubious collateral. If Paul's innate thuggishness hadn't alerted the shipper's agent, and then alarmed the prosecutor, we would have had no problem.

After that fiasco, I faced reality. Vestiges remained of the wine business I had run with Jean-Marie. Paul took over its security. As the goods moved only from one bonded warehouse to another, Paul mostly did paper work. When he left to join Hadad, we were both relieved.

What I hadn't noticed, in our two years together, was Paul's need for violence. The mistake was on the order of overlooking Margaret's need for stability. If I wanted to upset Gardel's plans, I couldn't hope for help from his chop boy, who had finally matched himself with the ideal boss.

At dusk I had gotten no further. Margaret brought in a small problem. I listened and nodded as my attention drifted. I have already mentioned that Exports Méditerranée makes few demands on me. The investments were carefully chosen over a number of years, and only one or two have given me any cause for regret. Four times a year, Margaret and I examine the results, expecting little from the managers except honesty and common sense. Even a small operating loss does not normally disturb me. It is difficult to sell large volumes of cement in Finland in January and unreasonable to demand a profit when prices are temporarily depressed. Neither circumstance lessens the value of a business with an established presence in its markets.

By analogy: The fact a mistress can be difficult from time to time does not make her less attractive.

She sat, knees forward, rump impatient, and finally said: "Well—what do we do?"

"Tell Leclerc it would be better if the next period is audited."

"No, about Captain Gardel. What do we do?"

Her stability was threatened, and she couldn't stand the uncertainty.

"For the time being, nothing."

"Nothing." She spoke quietly. Any of my wives would have exploded by now. Instead, Margaret considered the possibility I had a reason for inaction.

"He needs a lever," I said. "He hopes I will supply it."

"His lever is our lives."

"Which would work only until he used it."

"That reasoning will not protect us," she said calmly, "if he is impulsive or vindictive."

"He got to be an old man by acting carefully."

And brutally. I didn't say that.

She pressed. "He might decide to make an example of Jascha, or Suzy—or even Martino." Her fear wasn't only for them, of course.

"He's been careful not to harm anyone close to me. He doesn't want war. He wants submission." And if the old spider couldn't have what it wanted, it would happily leave behind drained husks. I didn't say that either.

Margaret stood. "I hope, patron, that you read him right."

"One more thing. Jean-Marie will call tomorrow. I'm not available. We are unable to accept the return of his investment."

She gave me a speculative look, wondering how much of that reversal was pointless cruelty.

Michael Weeks finally telephoned a few minutes after nine. He is a competent lawyer. Among his professional tricks is encouraging each client to feel incidental to the larger concerns of M. J. Weeks and therefore grateful when a call is returned, however late. The inevitable mistrust this invites—the inevitable question *Have Weeks's interests diverged from mine?*—has hurt his business over the years.

There were bistro noises in the background. I could imagine Michael setting up at Vagenende, napkin stuffed in his collar to the dismay of the waiters. In season he will consume two or three dozen Belons with a cheap Sancerre. He is large, dark-haired and rather slick-looking. He handles mostly criminal cases. I didn't employ him in setting up Exports Méditerranée , and he remains reproachful. That is my only explanation for his subsequent behavior.

Michael revels in his resentments, as only the English do. His father was a Liverpool merchant seaman; his mother claimed to be English but, in his cups Michael has confided she was most probably an Australian prostitute. It's indiscreet to mention such matters, but if this document is to have legal weight, the deeper contexts of each player are necessary. Michael, who will be my first reader, will attest to the accuracy of these details.

I let him run through the apology for not calling sooner, which was in fact his litany of all the things that had taken precedence.

I said, "Eric Laval showed up at lunch today."

Michael said something to the waiter—*Lafite 'soixante-et-une*—and to me, "If he has a valid reason, we should not discuss it on the phone."

"Apart from shaking me down, he can't have a reason."

"Good."

"But I want to know what reason he thinks he has. I want you to ask on my behalf."

"Duck before the bullet is fired, heh Charlie?" He chuckled. "Don't pay him anything before I get back to you."

I was deep in thought when the room ceased being a still life. Suzy crossed my field of vision, swung back a moment later, and before she could march past again, I said, "What is it?"

She stopped. She is tall for her age, mature only to the extent that young girls can be mature. If I'm distracted, I forget how little that means. She had her hair pinned back, picture of girlish innocence, and was wearing a T-shirt declaiming political drivel, tucked loosely into black tights, and was shuffling in old sandals. I was supposed to believe she wouldn't be caught dead going out like that. I expected a plea to relax the guard.

"He molested me," she said. She was barely audible.

"What?"

"He tried . . . to rape me."

I was stunned. For a moment I imagined her Italian in Hadad's condition, or impaled, or dismembered. But he hadn't gotten near her. As for the staff, it was inconceivable. I demanded: "*Who?*"

"Jascha."

"Jascha." I couldn't speak. I could barely control the shape of my face, which must have been turning red from the effort. Suzy's look, as she backed away, told me something awful was happening. I gasped, "Jascha! Oh, dear God! I should never have put him in charge of you. I will kill him."

Her face was crumpling now, but I didn't rush to comfort her. It's always better to get business done.

I made my tone as solemn as an executioner's. "Did he—?"

She bit her lip.

"—succeed, dear one?"

"No. Oh, no! He only—"

I beckoned. "Come here. You must tell me everything. Every detail. Then I will attend to what must be done. Martino will not enjoy helping me. Hugo will volunteer, I suppose, as he doesn't like Jascha."

Her face lost its last color. Instead of coming to me, she was trying to inch backward.

"I know you're shocked," I said, "but it is necessary. If only your honor were at stake—well, I don't know. But this is a matter of organizational discipline. Was this the first occasion?"

Close to panic. "*Yes!* No! It wasn't that—"

"So we are nipping the problem in the bud." I had pressed the button beside the desk drawer.

Jascha came in, cast barely a glance at Suzy. "Yes, patron?"

I snapped at him. "What instructions have I given you regarding the raping of your half-sister?"

"Patron—." He hesitated, looked at her, then said as if by rote, "You have said it is never permitted before sundown . . . unless she had been particularly obnoxious . . . and needs to be quieted down."

Her jaw dropped.

"Ah." Looking her in the eye, I said, "Suzy informs me that you attempted to rape her. She no doubt was being highly obnoxious, so you are forgiven."

"Yes, patron."

In a flash her dismay turned to rage. Her vocabulary of invective included both French and, regrettably, Italian. The substance of it was that I was not a father but a heartless jailer, and it might interest me to know that as far as Suzette Bourgeois Mistinguett was concerned, there was no longer any virtue to defend, the little dago having carried *that* off even if he'd had to leave her in captivity.

"So will you have *him* killed?" she cried.

Jascha watched with disgusted amusement. Before he could remind me that he was not a baby sitter, I shooed him out and offered my daughter a small glass of brandy.

"You shouldn't do such things," I said. "We must trust one another. And for reasons that do not concern you, I cannot relax security."

She sniffed across the rim of the glass. "You believed me for a moment."

"Until you mentioned your brother's name. He might die for you, but he would never harm you."

"I might die for him," she said.

My fault, tempting her with a chance at drama.

"All right. The two of you will die for each other."

She circled the office. "Would you die for Margaret?"

"I don't think that will be necessary."

"But would you?"

I pretended to consider. Not many days ago, I had been prepared to die to relieve boredom—not eager at the prospect but indifferent. Now annoyance had revived me. I felt disgusted by Paul and offended by Gardel. My survival instinct wasn't fully engaged, but I had begun taking minor precautions. As for dying on Margaret's behalf, the idea seemed distinctly unattractive. I enjoyed her company too much.

"A good assistant is worth several lives," I said, taking away Suzy's glass. A year ago she had made herself miserable reading Colette. I decided to have Margaret check her room for evidence of a relapse.

"You have no heart."

"I know."

When she left me alone, I toyed with another thought. Suzy's inspiration. A child feels free to tell the most implausible story, then feels cheated when an adult rejects the details that run counter to experience. *But,* protests the unformed mind, there *might* be dragons in the garden! Or, My brother *might* have tried to rape me! You can't *know* it didn't happen that way!

Yet one can, of course. The three-year-old lacks the perspective to appreciate not only that there are no dragons this afternoon but no dragons ever. The sixteen-year-old cannot appreciate how reliably character (her brother's or her own) defines possible actions.

This line of thought brought me to a question rather than an answer. Was I the one who lacked the fuller, adult perspective on murder— or was Carlos Gardel?

A man who had murdered often might also believe his garden harbored dragons, and that loving brothers raped sisters. An diseased mind could accept anything.

On the verge of sleep several hours later, Margaret Aznavourian confessed her certainty that my encounter with Gardel would end badly. "He will kill you, Charles," she whispered in the darkness, "and it will mean nothing to him."

9

The ear arrived Saturday morning in a carton large enough to have accommodated a head. There was an unnecessary note from Paul expressing his new patron's impatience.

I closed the box, gestured for its removal.

"This must be answered," Jascha said. His eyes were burning. "It must be answered in kind."

I nodded solemnly. "Whose ear do you propose to send?"

He looked at the carton in his hands. "Whose do you suppose this—?"

We found out an hour later, when a car delivered poor Hugo to the hotel's service entrance. No attempt had been made to bandage his head, against which he held a filthy and bloody rag. One of the security people had the presence of mind to alert Margaret. Another staffer distracted old Martino until his grandson was out of sight.

Margaret insisted on a hospital. Overruling her, I ordered Hugo brought upstairs, and in a silent fury at my coldness she summoned Dr. Bardo.

The youth sagged into a chair, tilted his head and inspected the rag. His eyes were dull. A spatter of blood ran diagonally like gunshot wounds across the front of his sleeveless undershirt. His muscular arms were filthy. There were hand-sized smears of blood on his forehead and one cheek. An eye was swollen half-shut. His cotton pants looked as if he'd been rolled under a bus. I told him the loss of an ear wouldn't make a difference, as he was already ugly enough to stop a hearse. He nodded.

I handed him a glass of marc. "When the doctor arrives," I said, "it's best he thinks you were in a bar fight. Okay?"

Mute nod.

"But you won't remember which bar."

Another nod. It would be a credible story. He looked as if he'd been in a week of bar fights, and his vacant expression told one and all he would have trouble remembering names. Suddenly he had an inspiration, removed the rag and showed Margaret the ear stub. The sight only increased her anger at me.

"He needs a hospital," she snapped. "You have no compassion."

Not that much for Hugo, it was true. He was neither intelligent nor particularly gentle toward anyone smaller than he, including his grandfather.

"Tell me what happened," I said.

His eyes lit up. "They fool me, say there's a cock fight up at Auribeau. They had a truck and we'd all go together. Then Paul climbs in the back and I know I was in the shit."

"Paul did—" I gestured.

"Real quick." He chopped the air with two fingers.

Bardo disinfected and bandaged the wound, left Cephalexin tablets with Margaret, who took Hugo down to his grandfather. Jascha paid Bardo excessively and came back wearing an idiotic grin. "The croaker believes Martino did it—and approves."

Margaret was silent when she returned. She did office busywork, she brushed off Jean-Marie as instructed, and when she couldn't stand it any longer, she said quietly, in a tone of exaggerated admiration, "So, mon coco, you certainly understand Captain Gardel. He would not harm anyone close to you—oh, no!—because he dreads Monsieur Mistinguett's declaration of war."

"You've never liked Hugo," I pointed out.

"What does that have to do with anything?" Her self-control was fraying. "I will tell you: nothing!"

"It may have," I said. My tone carried the confidence that she occasionally describes as smugness. "We tolerate Hugo because we love Martino, true enough? I think Gardel is aware of the distinction. He chose very carefully whose ear to amputate. He has shown he means business, but he does not have to go to bed tonight worrying about Jascha stealing through the garden with a silenced pistol."

Before she could say what was in her eyes—Perhaps he should—I added, "Suppose it had been you?"

"You would rationalize that as you do everything else," she said.

She knew better, but I don't like being blackmailed—not by Gardel, or the police, or a mistress—so I didn't reassure her.

Jascha and I took a walk on the beach. We weren't far from the hotel. Although the staff was alerted, I remained uneasy. They could keep most problems from coming in, but if Margaret took it into her head to go out, they would be powerless to stop her. The old woman who was overseeing Suzy was dim-witted and hopeless, unless the situation required shooting someone. So we kept the upper floor balconies in view and marched up and down near the water, like a couple of queers trolling for sandwich meat.

The boy thought he had calmed down, but his ideas were still bloody. "We must pull the old bastard's fangs, patron. A couple of the boys and I will do Paul. Then all you've got is an old Spaniard who stinks."

"No."

"The old man will not let go. Old people are like that. If they have money, they believe the world must bend to their wishes."

His lifetime's experience speaking.

"No."

"Captain Gardel hasn't hired first rate people. The closest he's come is Paul, who knows a few knife tricks. Without Paul, the others amount to nothing."

Not true, even the stupid Egyptians could be lethal. There also was a tactical reason for holding Paul off. Gardel and his men would be ready for an attack. Paul would be lying low. The Villa Balzar would have been made siege-proof.

He scuffed the sand. "Perhaps," he said mockingly, "the old man will die a natural death."

"If we mount adequate defenses, perhaps his interest will die," I said. I ordered him to tighten the watch on the hotel. No one would go out unaccompanied, except for Hugo if he wished to risk the other ear. "If Ali brings his boat back in the next few days, we will have a family outing—perhaps two or three weeks in the Canaries."

Suzy refused to accept the lockdown. "She threw a fit, even slapped Hilda," Jascha reported. "She states that dictators always wish to hide in bunkers."

"So do monks when the Saracens come raiding."

By evening, the moat was filled and the bridge raised. Jascha went out to inspect the perimeter. He came back twenty minutes later, looking smug. "The fat bastard was staking us out," he announced. "The one who pointed the knife at me? I shoved his teeth in and left him in a doorway."

"Wonderful," I said. "We'll have a war of attrition."

He skulked off.

I dined alone on the rear terrace. Margaret was in a poor temper.

10

"I don't need you, and I most certainly don't need your tantrums."

Edith Cerdan, Jascha's mother, proclaiming her sovereignty. She had said it often during our marriage, until she convinced herself the declaration was true and departed. She had been the only truly tall woman in my life. For a while I had thought this attribute would ensure a tranquil home. Tall people behave well, someone alleged, because they are so easily seen. Edith was unfamiliar with the maxim, or determined to demolish it. In her school years, she had upset the public mores by seducing the mayor of Menton. As she was fifteen and the daughter of a Communist hero of the Resistance, and he was in his mid-fifties and the emblem of bourgeois probity, the town could hardly pretend not to notice. When his wife attempted to stab the young mistress at a film opening, the affair ended and the scandal lost its charm. Edith and I had been married for several months before I heard of the episode.

She was never the movie starlet, as Jean-Marie would say, but always the confident leading woman. This afternoon she was repeating herself. "Your tantrums would drive away anyone, Charlie. I don't know why even the tart stays on your payroll."

Her son had taken her to lunch. She had come down from some Alps spa and was planning to drive to Paris tomorrow. In the meantime, a quick check on Jascha, a chance to wrinkle her nose at Margaret, and a chat with me about nothing at all. Oh, yes, and she wished to draw down a hundred thousand Euros.

"An expensive boyfriend?"

"No, I'm short of funds, that is all."

"It's only October, how can you be short?"

She shrugged. Expenses, what could she say?

"Well," I said, "let's see." I phoned Margaret-la-gigolette, who a minute later delivered a facsimile of Edith's account while pretending the woman didn't exist. I didn't need the piece of paper, but the busywork gave me time to consider the situation. It was unlikely Gardel was involved, so I could consider this a matter of Edith's habitual overspending. I studied the page and stared off into space for the mental computations that meant nothing, murmured to myself.

Finally, the bad news. "Here is the situation. You withdrew capital of forty thousand in March, and thirty in June. Last year we had earnings that, when divided among all the partners, equaled approximately a hundred twenty credited to your account. This year, as I'm sure I've mentioned, the business climate has not been favorable and we have little in profits to distribute. If you withdraw more than half of what you propose, you will be eating into your capital."

She stared, delicately bored.

"It's bad practice," I said.

"Please let's not be stuffy."

"And you may have to dip into capital next year anyway, unless things improve a great deal in the cement trade."

"So how much?"

"Twenty thousand would be prudent. Ten would leave a cushion for next year. And who knows—"

"Then I will take fifty, to show my confidence in your ability to do splendidly for us next year." After I'd asked Margaret to arrange the transfer, Edith said, "I'm grateful, Charlie, for the way you keep me out of trouble. Left to myself, I would spend every *balle* and die a poor old lady."

"You will die an old lady anyway, a very old one."

"But not a poor one, thanks to you."

"You're gracious today."

"I'm flush again. I may drive back to my spa for another week. Besides, your tantrum was not too bad. Sometimes, when I've said I needed money—"

"I know you're incurable. So I accept matters."

She blew through her lips. "You were much more fun when you were doing whatever it was that you were doing with that fat man, I forget his name. You had a sense of adventure. Now you must bore even yourself."

"I do sometimes," I said. Certainly she remembered Jean-Marie. We had shared too many summer afternoons, with Jean-Marie and his girl of the month, spending money as fast as we made it. There is a photograph that Jascha appropriated. It shows three friends grinning into the sun at an outdoor table in Cassis. Jean-Marie's girl must have taken it. The wine bottles are nearly empty, and the grins seem to me—twenty-some years later—to be idiotic. But Edith is beautiful and happy, so I understand why Jascha likes the picture. She knew then "whatever it was" that Jean-Marie and I were doing. There was a ready market along the Côte for Italian motor scooters, and ours—which came by eights and dozens over a mountain road, without paperwork—were duty-free.

"Your son says you lack flexibility," she said.

"Oh?"

"He describes you as mired in habit."

She had picked up on Jascha's uneasiness. Since she couldn't help, her curiosity promised only trouble.

"If he is insolent," I said, "I'll have to fire him."

She barely smiled. "He says you evade facts." When I didn't

pick up the bait, she gave up and asked, "Are you proud of him?"

"Extraordinarily." There was no need for fake enthusiasm. To Edith I could admit at least that one truth. My affection was rooted in pride. This may always be the case, whether we admit it or not.

"I'm off to Leysin," she said. She kissed my cheek quickly. "Come November, I think I'll spend a week in Champery, and ski the circuit. If you can get away, perhaps you should come up."

My reward, I understood, for being proud of our offspring.

"Call me if you decide," she said, and waved to Suzy on her way out. It was a long drive to the spa in the Vaud Alps. I knew I would not feel easy until Jascha had phoned her on some pretext in two days to see that she had arrived safely. That's a problem with having enemies. One worries excessively where they will strike.

Margaret waited nearly a half hour before coming in. "Fifty thousand?"

"I told her that over that amount, she would be eating into capital."

"She has no capital."

I shrugged.

"She spent it years ago."

I nodded.

"You are so clever," she said. Before I could agree, she added, "I hope not all your lies are expensive."

The police inspector Eric Laval didn't put a price tag on my lies. He had noticed what Edith had not, and his vanity made it impossible for him to keep silent. "Your security precautions suggest a guilty mind," he said.

Vanity! The word doesn't describe a man who admires every whisker in his beard.

"A guilty mind," he repeated, as if he had hit upon a clue.

Police stations tend to be well-fortified, their denizens well-armed, presumably not because of guilty minds. I could have pointed this out, but I wasn't in a mood for thrust and parry. Being interviewed by a policeman was a stressful way to begin a Monday morning, after a difficult weekend surrounded by sulky people. Worse, I had gotten no response from my lawyer.

I sat straight behind my desk and said, "Miss Aznavourian said you had business."

"The varieties of crime along the Riviera. . . ." He tilted his head, leaving the thought dangling, as if it were worth close inspection. He was a man without subtlety, without much intelligence, though he would never have accepted this description. It was obvious he had prepared a speech and would be frustrated if he could not deliver it. "It keeps a policeman busy. Car theft—where do they all end up? And the lowly pickpocket—the Gypsy pipsqueak who would be inconsequential in Paris, or perhaps would have his fingers broken—in St. Trop, or Cannes, or Menton this flea is stealing a half-million in a summer. And the prostitution! It is not enough that the Russian and Romanian trash has overrun Paris; their keepers spread them along the Croisette like pigeon shit. The pimps sprinkle them on yachts, dangle them from balconies. It is so much to keep up with! A policemen cannot simply ignore these matters that are so much in the open! It makes one grateful when crime is done discreetly, so it need not be noticed."

I glanced vaguely at my desk, as if business awaited.

"The more sophisticated criminals," Laval went on, "run quiet, seemingly respectable operations. If they are good, a poor dumb cop can't even figure out what crime is being done. Technology smuggling? Money laundering? Too slick for all but the most modern policeman. Did I tell you? I myself am a traditionalist. If there are no problems disturbing the public, why should I create them?" He raised a hand, moued his lips. Why indeed?

I refused to be drawn in. It's in the cops' handbook that they must control each encounter. This means defining the terms, inviting the person being interrogated to step onto their turf. Firmly, I said, "Surely you came with business in mind?"

Vain people have many sensitive spots that one need only touch to observe a twitch. Laval's official carnet assured him he was to be in charge. I had refused to accept his terms. He had been wearing out my rug, wandering a few feet this way, a few that, to accompany his reflection. Now he took two steps closer to my desk. He couldn't prevent his eyes from narrowing in annoyance.

"You are wrong, m'sieu. I have no business purpose. The call is professional, of course, but with no particular point."

His visit definitely had a purpose, and I needed to know what it was. Games of bluff against *flics* are difficult, because they can make trouble for you that you cannot make for them. A policeman need reveal his hand only when he pleases, and in the meantime his victim can only worry!

So it became my turn to make conversation. I said, "Your wife is rather unattractive." The actual phrase was stronger: *remede contre l'amour*, which was saying she would put you off sex.

"My wife is quite ugly. But the woman with whom you saw me is not my wife. She is with the tax authority. In her way, she is most unusual. Stupid people are the most dedicated. She is both dedicated and intelligent."

I got up and stomped around a bit, complaining about taxes, Paris, Socialists, Gaullists, and Greens, none of them ever satisfied with enough. Before I could get going on the unions, Inspector Laval interrupted.

"What have you heard recently about the Hadad gang?" he asked.

I pretended puzzlement. Hadad. Hadad. I muttered, "Their leader is a madman. You must know that already."

"One of your people has gone to work for him. The Chinese kid."

"You mean Paul. He hasn't been with me for several years."

"But he still works for Hadad?"

"I wouldn't know."

"I'm surprised."

"Hadad and I are neither partners nor competitors, you understand, so there is no contact."

He made a noise that could have meant anything. "Hamilton Hadad Adid's case would surprise the average criminologist," he said. "Many street thugs rise in their criminal milieu, but they have additional talents beyond brutishness. As far as I can determine, Hadad has none."

Were we keeping him alive on pretense, I wondered, or were the body and head still decomposing beside the highway?

"He has a reputation as a molester of young men," I offered.

"You don't like him very much."

"The Côte's criminal population is not my concern."

"No, m'sieu, I must disagree. It is every citizen's concern. Unless—" he smiled "—the crime is out of sight."

"Hadad's crimes, if any, are out of my sight. If he's stirring things up—" I shrugged. I couldn't bring myself to say anything about the excellent police agencies restoring order, how I was certain this would quell any Hadad mischief, et cet. I walked to the server and selected a good bottle of Scotch whiskey. I couldn't fathom his interest in Hadad, unless the body had been found. Even then, if he had made any inquiries at all, he would know that Paul hadn't been on my payroll for years; he couldn't suspect Hamilton had been killed on my order. But perhaps that wouldn't matter. A policeman can fasten on the most absurd idea and never let go.

I opened the Scotch. "Would you like a drink?"

"Wouldn't mind." For some reason he was pleased with himself.

"What *is* Hadad up to?" I said.

"I thought I told you." He chortled into his glass.

"No, you didn't."

"No, I did. I told you it was too complicated for a stupid policeman to understand. He has quite a little empire. Incredible what such a primitive brute can accomplish. It's like finding an amoeba writing poetry. A rebuke, in any case, to the life of a civil servant, don't you agree?"

I thought of Gardel's cheap cynicism concerning civil servants. The Spaniard would have sneered that Laval had not learned the possibilities of his office; that the crimes of the political class made Hamilton Hadad's rackets trivial.

"You can arrest Hadad," I said. "That is a more severe rebuke."

"Ah, I may! At the moment, the little immigrant is difficult to find. You know nothing of his whereabouts? His Chinese enforcer has been seen around, as have a few of the regular goons. But of Hadad—nothing. I'm certain he will turn up with a new scheme. Then I will arrest him—and perhaps you, if you're in business together."

"I can assure you—"

"And we know what the assurance would be worth." He set down his glass, not out of principle; the thing was empty. "Personally, I do not care what you do as long as I don't have to see it. Perhaps you do not collaborate with Hadad. Perhaps you still compete, and that is why blood has been spilled."

My stomach twisted, and a bubble of gas banged my heart. So he knew.

"You're surprised." Chin rising, he relished another triumph. "You shouldn't be. When one of your goons comes home missing an ear, the police hear. It is exactly the sort of thing that compels us to take notice."

I took a breath.

The police should do everything possible, I said, to suppress violence at rooster fights. I got Inspector Laval out of the suite, cursing myself for a fool. If this *flic* got the chance, he would happily lay Hadad's head at my door.

Panic is not my usual response. I admit that I came close that afternoon to summoning Jascha for a drive up the N85 to remove evidence. Two thoughts deterred me. One was that the police could be waiting. The other: Even if I found the exact spot where Paul had dumped Hadad, I had no idea what to do with the pieces. However Laval construed things, the corpse was less incriminating where it lay than in my possession.

It was tempting, nonetheless. Imagining Gardel opening his carton a few minutes before the police arrived—yes, that was tempting indeed.

Michael Weeks called before noon. "You don't have to duck a bullet, Charlie," he announced with high confidence. The background was quite for a change. It was possible he was in his office. "Eric Laval has been promoted to investigate matters with political implications. You haven't been dabbling in narcotics, have you?"

"Of course not."

"What about espionage? Or selling machine guns? No, you wouldn't. I always wonder: who needs guns who doesn't already have them?"

"It's very interesting, what you wonder," I said, "only not useful to me. Tell me more about Laval."

"I told you what I know. He has risen in the ranks. You're not on his beat anymore."

Two hours earlier, the man on whose beat I wasn't had been drinking my Scotch and making threats.*

"Laval came to visit me this afternoon, asking about Hamilton Hadad Adid."

The lawyer made an unpleasant sound. "Are you holding back on me, old horse?"

I've never cared much for the Englishman's repertoire of endearments: old sport, old horse, little heart, old fruit. I don't recall precisely which he used but believe it was old horse, old dear spavined client.

"No, Michael."

"No little sidelines while the plastic pipes business is slack?"

---

*Of what use is a lawyer who is too lazy to make more than one telephone call? It is beyond dispute that Michael Weeks's negligence contributed to my problems. If I had not had to act for so long on incomplete information, I would have acted differently. And the steps I took would be seen in a better light.

"It's cement that's slow this year."

"No important clients who feel you've cheated them?"

"I have partners, not clients. And they're all happy."

He snickered. "They haven't much choice, have they?"

"I deal fairly with all of them," I said.

"One of these days, someone will get fed up with your fair treatment, Charlie. You'll be lucky if they only send policemen after you."

This was resentment talking. Except for a coward named Jean-Marie, all the partners appreciate what I've done for them. Even poor hopeless Edith, especially Edith.

Having watched an ex-wife and a policeman come and go in two days, Margaret had run out of diplomatic tact by that evening. She waved a sheet of stationery in my face, like a waiter presenting an overdue bill. "Tell me the truth, Charles! Did you murder Yves Bulant?"

11

"Time provides no sanctuary for the murderer. Justice will be rendered without favor, at midnight as readily as at noon."

Who had said all that the first time? A man confident of his eye for guilt. Robespierre, perhaps.

"The blood of Yves Bulant cries out for justice against Charles Mistinguett!"

I handed Margaret the page. "This came in the mail?"

"It was addressed to me. Who is Yves Bulant. Did you murder him?"

"Why, *chouchoute*, you see it there, written plainly. Well, not plainly, but clearly. Bulant's blood cries out for—what was it? Oh, yes, for justice."

There were tears in her eyes, and I should have relented. But the recent days had taken a toll on my nerves. Any moment I expected Laval to accuse me of running a street corner *boucherie* for punks. My mistress was ready to accuse me of hacking—or shooting, garroting, whatever!—an oversexed friend thirty years ago. I put on a calm face, which made matters worse. "He has noisy blood, according to your correspondent. Who, by the way, appears to be Senor Gardel."

"Who, by the way, appears to know things about you that I don't."

I shrugged. "We have a different relationship, Gardel and I."

For several seconds she stared at me in silence, thinking she saw—I don't know what—a cold monster, I suppose, capable of murdering a man and distancing a mistress, as circumstances required. I can't blame her. The strain had affected us both. She craved stability, and had settled for less of it than most women demand. Now she saw that I wasn't what she believed me to be, and the emotional tether connecting us was dissolving. I can't say I was without regret. But it should have dissolved earlier if she had so little confidence in me.

The practical Margaret took over. "He's threatening you with the police, patron. Would he have evidence?"

"Would the police require evidence?" I asked. "Yves Bulant was my first wife's lover. You know how long ago that was. Whatever happened, there will be no evidence."

"Did you murder your wife as well?"

I could have reminded her that she had only Gardel's word on Bulant. Instead I said, "It seemed pointless." Pointless because Mireille had been my mistake—why hold it against the woman? A mistake once recognized is seven-eighths repaired.

"Perhaps now you wish you had."

My thinking had taken the same turn. No insurmountable chore for Gardel to have learned of my former wives. Ham Hadad might have known something of Mireille and shared it, depending on how long he and Gardel were partners. Jean-Marie knew everything. If the Spaniard had tracked down Mireille, he would have gotten an earful. What the old man wouldn't know was that Mireille had told the same stories to the Paris police thirty years ago. What the *flics* couldn't prove when the corpse was fresh—if only it could be found!—wouldn't excite them today.

"Nothing can be proved against me," I said.

"You find it amusing?"

"I admit it."

"Then you have not thought very hard. Even if the crime cannot be proven, the police can make your life miserable. Do you really want some little sneak inspecting your mail, tapping into your computers, interviewing the staff, visiting when he feels like it? Do you want Laval asking insinuating questions of your partners? How many hundreds of small regulations do your imagine our hotel may be breaking?"

"Not many. The management is professional."

"You are still smiling! What's the matter with you?"

"Read that letter again, cheri. Gardel is dredging up a lurid old tale to whip me into line. When an adversary threatens you with the police, it's because he has run out of other ammunition. That's why I'm smiling. Also, because the tale happens to be untrue."

Normally she would have smiled back, but now she was businesslike. She unfolded the letter, placed it on the sofa beside me. "I see no reference, patron, to the police. He mentions blood, he mentions justice. Your friend said Gardel rejects true, abstract justice but takes pleasure in imposing his own kind. I believe the old man is warning you—warning us—that if you remain difficult his sense of justice will overwhelm other considerations."

I stared at the note, considering. It had seemed so absurd, a floridly threatening letter.

"That is why," Margaret went on, "we must consider what is to be done about General Guiot."

"Nothing is to be done."

"Then—" accepting with that dreadful female pragmatism my role as assassin "—it is your life or Carlos Gardel's."

She is not normally bloodthirsty. And by temperament she was ill-suited to urging murder in the name of necessity. She knew nothing of Hadad's carving. Yet she was right, Gardel had me boxed. He could use the police to hamper my movements. He could strike as if he were God's hand when it suited him.

Her chin was up. "Gardel likes young women."

The grim drape of her mouth, the wounds in her eyes—she couldn't love me any longer, they admitted, but, before we went our separate ways, she would serve in the campaign against Gardel. No sacrifice would be unthinkable. So she would offer herself.

All very fine, but unnecessary.

I took a turn around the perimeter. The defenses were satisfactory, assuming the defenders could be trusted. On the outside, within a block, I saw two of Hadad's Egyptians lurking clumsily in doorways, Laval's plump *hausfrau* slumped in a parked car, with a radio plug in her ear, and a sub-Saharan character dressed in running shoes and a linen suit, hanging out at the hotel's east bar. The two groups were unaware of each other.

I got a taxi at the front door and took a direct route to Jean-Marie Gassion's hotel. As I entered the lobby, the *hausfrau* and her driver were pulling to the curb half a block away and a Mercedes with darkened windows was trying to look inconspicuous as it cruised past.

I went through the lobby in a hurry. Out the rear door, past a booming disco, up an alley—and Jascha was already there, in the Lancia, with an overnight bag in the back. He dropped me at the rail station. The coastal train got me down to Marseilles in plenty of time to connect with the evening TGV to Paris.

I had no intention of becoming an assassin. I repeated that mantra. Gardel could not force me to become an assassin.

12

André Guiot appeared to be a man of habit. In the morning a private car drove him from an expensive suburb to the office. At six-thirty or six-forty-five in the evening, the car left the office building's gated courtyard, presumably with Guiot aboard, and sped toward the ring road. I followed him from his home to the office on Tuesday morning and repeated the trip in reverse that evening. On Wednesday we did it all again. I glimpsed him only four times in those two days, as he entered or left the car at his home. He was an undistinguished as a man can be without disappearing. He had no trace of military bearing. He was in his fifties, quite trim, with white hair combed straight back from a low and narrow forehead. The eyebrows were perhaps heavy — I noticed that on Thursday morning — and the lips a bit full. There had been a Slav somewhere in the family tree. But you wouldn't pick Guiot out of a crowd by any of those features, and the sum of them equaled anonymity.

Security was evident all around Paris. Soldiers lurked outside the Métro stations. Trash cans had been sealed. A cadre of Algerians, displeased by France's meddling in their election, had planted bombs at a flower mart and the Place Vendome.

I kept in touch with Jascha. Several times a day he assured me all was quiet. Several times I called back to ask again. Twice I vetoed sending Martino out to Villa Balzar for surveillance.

"When are you coming home?" Jascha asked.

"Soon."

"Have you learned anything?"

"The general would be easy to kill."

"No, boss—"

I hung up on his alarm. I had become a regular at Monte Cristo. Veal, glass of Chianti, no dessert. A few doors down was a puppet shop. I made a pest of myself shopping for a grandson. On either side of the narrow street were art galleries, wine shops, small and expensive restaurants. It wasn't difficult to spend a day in that little neighborhood. Midway along, on a cross-street, Rue des Deux Ponts, I found I could walk a block in either direction without losing sight of traffic on the main drag.

I was so attentive to the general's car that he nearly escaped on foot. It was Thursday toward noon, and I had worn out every welcome along the main street. I had avoided the shops and was perched on the wall at Quai de Bourbon above the Seine when I saw the general in the street a block south. By the time I got into line behind him and his two bodyguards, who followed at a discreet distance, we were crossing a bridge to the city's other main island.

We walked the length of the larger island. When Guiot strode into Place Dauphine, I thought his destination was one of the restaurants that line two sides of the triangular park. But he kept going, crossed a busy road connecting the right and left banks, descended a steep flight of stairs, and strolled toward the island's downstream point. I wondered if it was coincidence that a retired general's exercise led him to the exact spot where the Templars' Jacques de Molay was incinerated in the Fourteenth Century. An officer who had not known combat might prize heroic moments.

The park, well below street level and close to the water, was getting a chill breeze. Guiot trod the gravel paths, the wind on his back, seeming to take mild interest in the lovers, artists and aging *Figaro* readers with no further purpose. The guards stopped at a swinging metal gate at the head of the park. Their bearing was altogether military; young men with alert eyes and wide stances.

Guiot had come for a rendezvous. He sat on a bench, and he and the man who had been waiting faced the river with its slow-moving barges. The other man wore a topcoat, the raised collar ruffled in the wind. The conversation was brisk, without the eye contact or shoulder-shifting of old friends comparing the quality of their lives to date.

The other man had been sitting when Guiot arrived, so it was impossible to tell much about him. He looked neither tall nor short, but he could have been either; the bulky coat hid clues from his posture. The hair was light, more blond than gray. The skin was pale. The river light was on his face, which I could glimpse only in profile. A long sharp nose shadowed a trim mustache.

There was something loudly clandestine in the meeting. If they had sat together at a Boule Miche cafe, it would have been far less noticeable.

I was paying attention to a pair of girls sketching the downriver vista of the Pont des Arts and the Louvre. Both drawings had the feel of the river and its light flowing out of the city. If you were left behind, you might feel a little sad. I looked over their shoulders until the girls became suspicious, and by then Guiot had left and his companion had produced a bag of crumbs for the pigeons.

Guiot's social life wasn't related to my problem. Nor was his business life—except the little part of it that had upset Gardel.

I climbed to the street and sat on a bench on the bridge and waited.

The man who had waited for Guiot was taller than I had expected, and he walked with more determination than the average middle-aged Frenchman. I expected him to hail a taxi or dip into the Métro. But he walked, shouldering through the lunchtime crowd, and before long we were on Rivoli on the right bank and then something in his arrogance made the rest almost inevitable. At the flabby seat of the Republic, Élysée Palace, he strode past the guards with a brisk salute.

Reasonable enough. The retired general Guiot retained some contact with a government functionary, who had an office in the president's palace. Perhaps a contract for more war games was in the works. Perhaps—since war wasn't in prospect in Western Europe this fall—they had other business and thought it better to meet secretly. Perhaps, perhaps.

I took up my station at Monte Cristo. A long lunch would help the mind, a bottle of Chianti would help the digestion. There were tables beside the windows, which I avoided. I preferred a banquet midway back. The gates of Guiot's building were perfectly visible. I could sit and wonder how a retired general spends his work days. As a director of a bank and a steel company, he would have documents to review, meetings to attend; those duties would occupy a small part of a productive man's time. There must be a business of Guiot's own, but the building gave no clue to its nature. Perhaps Guiot and his guards spent the afternoons on their bellies and elbows, pushing toy tanks over imaginary terrain in search of enemies.

Watching the street, I didn't pay attention to what was going on inside the restaurant. A man came down the steps from the bar that occupies the bistro's second story. He was in my peripheral vision all the way. But even when he whipped a chair away from the table and sat facing me, recognition took a moment. The fat Egyptian had fewer teeth than he'd had at the outset of my first drive to meet Gardel. There were ugly scabs where the lips were healing. I am good at names. Paul Chen had called this Neanderthal Munifal. His scrawny friend came down the steps and stood behind the chair. Gafar.

"Where's your keeper?" I said.

"I don't have a keeper."

"Your friend from Marseilles."

Munifal looked uncomfortable. "Paul gave him a chance, but he wouldn't switch teams." Paul's name came with reverence.

"Where's Paul?" Had to be nearby.

Munifal shrugged.

"Come on. He isn't crazy enough to let you imbeciles off the leash."

"Shut up."

The waiter brought my pasta, filled my glass, asked the Egyptians if they were eating. Munifal waved him off. "Neither is this shit. We have business." He opened his jacket so I could see the automatic pistol stuck in the top of his pants. Unfortunately so could the waiter. "Bring him the check."

I took a forkful of pasta. To the waiter: "There's no rush." To the seated man: "One of you had better get Paul before you screw up. Guns in the hands of monkeys don't frighten me."

It was only half bravado. However dearly Munifal wanted to even the score for the beating Jascha had inflicted, he was obviously intimidated by Paul. If Paul hadn't told them to shoot me, given a choice they wouldn't. I wondered what surgery he'd performed on the thug from Marseille.

"So where is Paul?" I said.

I had an inkling. If the young Chinese appeared from across the street, planted a knife dripping Guiot's blood on the table in front of me, a dozen witnesses would be available against me. A dozen in Monte Cristo plus the puppet shop owner and everyone who had seen me staking out Guiot's building.

Munifal held his ragged grin.

Losing patience, I threw the wine in his face.

It was only half a glass, not enough to keep an otherwise devout Muslim out of Paradise. If he hadn't insisted on giving me that open-mouthed grin, he wouldn't have swallowed a spoonful. He hurled himself back from the table, bumping the skinny one, reaching for his gun. The waiter ran for cover.

I remained seated. "Bring Paul here," I said. "I'm not coming to him. Bring" —*pat*, I slapped the table between words—"him (*pat*) to (*pat*) me."

There had been a time, before the disintegration of French culture under the immigration, when hired muscle could be relied on to take instruction. In those days, a Munifal—whose name would have been something French—would never have thought of shooting a man he had not been ordered to shoot. Munifal thought hard about it before remembering it was Paul Chen giving orders. He pushed the automatic back into his pants. Without wiping his face, the told the skinny one to watch me and left the restaurant.

In Marseilles, a proprietor with good sense doesn't call the police every time he glimpses a handgun. In Paris these days, who knew? I gave the waiter an extravagant tip and a romantic story. Then I persuaded the scrawny Egyptian to go after Munifal. "Just send Paul to me, Gafar. If the waiter sees your friend again, he'll call the *flics*."

"He'll kill you."

"He's going to get you killed."

"We'll *both* kill *you*."

Neanderthal solidarity. I made a brushing motion and he went. It was too late for me to run. Too many eyes had witnessed the scene. Italians appreciate a commotion much more than the French, who look askance; at least half Monte Cristo's patrons were Italian. If the waiter passed around my story—that I'd seduced a policeman's wife—they might have a quiet laugh and forget. Provided nobody had been murdered across the street.

I waited for Paul.

If he hadn't done the job, I could talk him out of it. His apes had drawn too much attention. Better to wait a day. We'd *all* been noticed, not merely I. Etc.

I saw him pass twice on the other side of the street. He couldn't see into the restaurant, which was darker than the afternoon street. When he finally came inside, he was jumping with excitement. The other patrons noticed. First two thick-skulled Egyptians. Now a buzzy-eyed Chinese.

I stood and waved him over. He had a wild spring in each step. It didn't carry him as high as the ceiling, but even when he sat he seemed to be bobbing a few inches into the air.

"You're full of surprises, boss man. Did you come up here to help with the job?" His finger became a gun aimed across the street. His voice dropped. "The ear thing got your attention, huh? Must really piss you, taking orders from your old laundry boy. I had to hold myself back on the ear. Once you've started cutting, you just want to keep going."

"You should be a surgeon."

"I could perform surgery on your tongue." He thought about it. "Or on your boyfriend's dick."

"I'll count myself warned."

His fingers were twitching on the table cloth. "Why did you come up here?"

"To warn Guiot."

"The old man won't like that."

"Screw him."

"He'd want me to do you right here."

"You're not that nuts yet."

"There isn't much I wouldn't do. Like Guiot. I was thinking of good ways to get him—figuring you weren't going to help, you know? A kilo of Semtex in that limo, maybe in the bar. He opens it for a drink—bam!—blows his guts out the trunk. A bomb makes a statement."

"In any language," I agreed. He was, I thought, *that* nuts. His deterioration touched me, because I had once thought him promising. The Egyptians were simple souls, willing to kill me on orders, handy helpers on Paul's other executions, afraid as if they'd been carrying a lethal snake around in a bag.

"Paul—," I began, then stopped. What could I say? It was too late for bromides about coming to his senses. He amputated ears only as a shortcut to heads. Having found himself, he could never go back to being a laundry boy. "What does the Spaniard have against Guiot?"

He leaned back, pretending to lose interest. "The old man is wicked. He should be running a triad. There's a problem? *Chop*, it's gone. *Chop!* That is Guiot's future. Dead man."

"Gardel said he'd refused a proposal."

"Could be." He shrugged. "Like Hamilton. Like you."

"If I help you with Guiot, I won't be in a position to refuse anything."

"You're not anyway. You're vulnerable, wide open. It's taking you a long time to realize it. Senor Gardel wants you working on the inside, like a partner."

"Shaking down friends."

"You've done it before."

I said, "Is Gardel trying to extort money from Guiot?"

He shrugged again, and I wondered what lever Gardel had tried to use before deciding Guiot should be murdered. I had told the old man the truth about scandals in France. Indignation is reflexive and short-lived, and humiliating private matters are never discussed. If Gardel had photographs of the President of the Republic in a lace brassiere, no publication would buy them or use them. Francois Mitterrand acknowledged his illegitimate daughter before Canal 5 did.

"Have a brandy, Paul."

"Volvic," he said.

The waiter braved another visit, and we had our bottles of water in a few seconds.

"It isn't disloyal, Paul," I began cheerfully, "to hedge a bet just a little. It seems to me you are in the dark about much of Gardel's plan. You're taking him on faith. When you worked for me, I never asked you to do that. Even when you went to Hong Kong, you had the full picture."

Absolutely untrue, but there was no way he could know. My point in any case was fair. He had not operated totally in the dark. I had never sent him out like a windup toy with orders suitable to a Munifal: Bribe this man, maim that one. Respecting his intelligence had meant overestimating it.

"Guiot worked in Africa, I know that much." When I remained unimpressed, Paul added: "Gardel was in North Africa. I don't think he had a network, but you know Africa: everybody screwing around, watching everybody else doing it. The French are everywhere, not just on your old turf. Remember

Emperor Bokassa, who liked to eat children? He wasn't there by accident or because he'd won an election. France installed him, and he was grateful and let President Giscard fuck one of his wives. So France poured a few billion into the place, the Central African Republic, and Bokassa was more grateful. He stuffed Giscard's pockets with diamonds."

"That scandal is thirty years old," I said.

"Guiot was there, too."

"In Africa?"

"I'm telling this. The old man doesn't tell me any of this. He tells one of the girls he's got hanging around, just reminiscing, like it's the most fascinating thing in the world, the exploits of Don Gardel, and she's just listening to get a hit of coke. Now that I boss security for the old man, I get to hear a lot of things. What happened in Africa was, the old man was doing his usual listening, just had an ear cocked, he tells the girl. Israelis were thick on the ground in Central Africa, trying to make friends, and one cell gets the skinny on Giscard. And the Spaniard hears because he's got an Israeli friend under cover in Tunis. So the story hits in Paris, and it finishes off Giscard."

"Gardel leaked the story?"

"He didn't have anything to do with it. Telling people their president is a crook isn't the old man's style. Dirt is useful, he says, only till it's out in the open. But his little Israeli bird says Guiot arranged the diamonds. About the black pussy, I don't know. A couple of generals got rich back then. Today they're big shots. Guiot owns part of a bank. You can figure what the Spaniard has in mind. But Guiot would rather be dead than pay a few Euros."

"Have you leaned on any of the others?"

"There are two besides Guiot. We gave one the bad news and he laughed at us. So you see, killing Guiot will be a useful *publicité*. We will explain to number two, and he will tell the third." He lifted his palms, as if everything that would follow was obvious: prominent men with military backgrounds would pay eagerly, once they understood the alternative.

"Why won't they just have you and Gardel buried?"

"The old man is invisible. None of them knows who made the touch." He opened a screwball grin. "After Guiot is taken care of, we may approach the survivors as Exports Méditerranée. If they react badly, they can kill you."

It's possible to reason with a madman, if one accepts his points of reference. In a tone of utter pragmatism, I said, "If you kill enough important people, Gardel won't stay invisible. Suppose you blow up Guiot's automobile. The anti-terrorism bureau would investigate. They have all the resources of the government, including measures as illegal as your own. Think about that."

Leaning back from the table, he giggled. "You talk like an old woman. *'Ooh, we don't want to make the flics mad, Paul.'* Unless you squeal, nobody will tell the *flics* Gardel is directing the show."

"There are Hamilton Hadad's thugs."

"They don't talk."

"Don't be sure," I said. "A policeman came around a few days ago asking questions. Nominally he was interested in Hadad's operations. He mentioned you. From Hadad to you to Gardel is only two steps."

His glance came up from below. "What did you tell him?"

"I let him talk. But instinct tells me he smells Gardel." I gave it a beat of three. "It's an argument for not killing anyone right now."

"Capitán Gardel is right. You would eat a plateful of shit every day to save your ass. Are you going to get the job done?"

"I want more time. If I kill someone," I said pragmatically, "I want to get away with it."

Quite simply, I could not trust Michael Weeks to handle the matter. I phoned Margaret from a public box. She went down to the hotel's Negritude bar, from which she called me back.

My objectives were limited. First, I wanted to pass a discreet warning to General Guiot. Despite mixed parentage, my attitude in such things as corruption is completely French: no man deserves a death sentence for the ordinary vices. But I had to approach Guiot with a credible introduction. A man who is accosted by a stranger warning of imminent doom is likely to be casual about the warning, and careless about revealing its source. If that was my only option, Guiot was on his own. But I hoped that our circles of acquaintances might overlap. I told Margaret to begin getting in touch with our partners.

"Yes, patron." She hesitated. The strategic pause was one of her techniques for preparing me. Typically: *Charles —*, hesitation. If there has been a sin of omission, I ask to be told its nature. If there is bad news, I ask to hear it. I always fulfill my part in the ritual. It's dangerous not to know what's on a woman's mind.

"Is there something more?" I said.

"That ugly woman who was with Laval has returned. She has an assistant. They're making a nuisance of themselves at the hotel's office, demanding records."

"Is Robert cooperating?"

"Yes."

"All right then."

"They are in the computer files."

"Let them. The hotel owes no unpaid taxes." Before she could say *yes but,* I added, "I'm certain Robert has hundreds of files to show them."

I walked back to the tiny Rue de l'Hotel-Colbert. In retirement, Mitterrand had lived just around the corner. Or perhaps it was his mistress. Across the street from the hotel was a restaurant with a good cellar. It was a place I would have enjoyed bringing Margaret if the trip had been for pleasure. Two bottles of eighty-six Beychevelle and Francois's roast young duck would take the mind off most troubles.

So Laval was putting pressure on me. The dedicated, intelligent, ugly woman would find nothing in Robert's computers to help tax collectors or the police. But her arrival convinced me that Laval was serious. So his interest wasn't in Hadad, not Hadad alive or dead, and not Mistinguett. Laval had gotten a whiff of larger game. His patter about discreet crime not bothering him was sheer flummery. Discreet crime would interest him most. It would pose a worthy challenge to his supposed investigative skills. Why had I imagined a policeman would tell the truth?

There was a store selling musical instruments on the corner. As I admired the unfinished pieces of a violin, I saw a familiar shape behind me on the quay. It was the fat idiot, pretending interest in a bookseller's material. So Paul had had me followed.

I strolled up the street and into the hotel, allowing Munifal time to cross the busy avenue. They would be less worried if they knew where I slept. I had a pastis in the tiny lounge and went upstairs for a nap. By seven-thirty I was back downstairs having another drink. Margaret had awakened me by phoning with the information I needed. "I made an appointment for you, patron," she said.

I could see the sidewalk and the pipestem street, both shiny with rain that was still falling. There wasn't room for a parked car, and neither of Paul's Egyptians occupied nearby doorways. He might have put surveillance further in the background. He would be afraid of losing track of me.

I borrowed an umbrella and walked to the Métro station at Place St.-Michel. Every few minutes the rain stopped, and pedestrians immediately filled the streets and jammed the cafe tables. The lighted fountain was aswarm with teenagers. When Jean-Marie Gassion and I were running taxi cabs, I earned my first penicillin needle with a chance acquaintance from Place St.-Michel.

I made a perfunctory effort at spotting a tail. If Paul had more of his muscle in the field, they would expect a little neck-craning. I supplied it.

When I changed trains at Odeon I made a production of looking at the station map and then double-checking and triple-checking after I'd switched to the Boulogne-bound line. Here was a man having a hard time finding a route to his destination. A moment before the train pulled out of Odeon, I leapt off the fold-down seat, cast a panicked look at the map, and dashed from the car. Gafar, at the other end of the carriage, had no chance to follow.

When I reached the street, I was only a few blocks from my rendezvous.

Leonid Kargman, a small, seedy publisher of magazines, had been one of my partners for twenty years. He had chosen a Russian restaurant for our meeting because he liked zakouski and pepper vodka. His nose was a wrinkled plum, his eyes tiny and dark. Motioning me to sit, he said without preamble: "Guiot is wary of strangers. He insisted I satisfy myself before he meets you."

"I see," I said.

"Of course, I am satisfied already. Your request was enough."

"Thank you."

"You needn't take that tone. Mademoiselle Aznavourian was vague, and suddenly Guiot is afraid of strangers. That is almost as surprising as your returning to Paris." He raised his glass. "Salud, Charles! I thought you had sworn it off."

"Except for business; this is business."

"Yes, about that—"

"I need to see Guiot."

He poured vodka from a carafe. "The zakouski are excellent. And Riga sprats are the very best, yes?" He nibbled on a morsel of fish.

"What worries Guiot?" I said.

"He's not saying, to me. Perhaps it is these unsettled times. Too many of our foreign adventures have borne poisoned fruit. You know of the bombings? Of course you do. As I told Mademoiselle, I do not know Guiot closely. Several years ago, when my reputation was better, I was able to help him find a publisher for a bit of military history he had written. An émigré friend introduced us. Now we are in touch twice a year, over transgressions by his publisher. He expected his treatise on

Bordino to capture the public imagination." He choked on the vodka. "So you see, Charles, Guiot's confidence in my word is limited. As to your business, if you could describe it to me so that I may—"

"Leo! What have you told him about me?"

"Nothing, virtually nothing. A prominent man is approached by many people, and he must—"

"Leo, get him on the telephone. Tell Guiot that I do not wish to offer him an investment opportunity, or to revisit old scandals, or to represent the people who have threatened him. Tell him they are not my friends. Tell him you know I am as good as my word."

The old man's eyes closed slowly and opened. Acknowledgment or suffering.

"Are you sleepy from the vodka?" I asked.

"No, Charles." For a moment he sat with hands folded on the table. "I will go in a minute. Could you tell me, perhaps, how my investment is doing?"

"Cement is slow. It will remain slow this year, unless they build another Chunnel. So our income will be small. Next year things will be better."

"I'm not a young man. If I can't spend it this year, I may never get to do so."

Edith's thinking, exactly, though she couldn't claim age.

"And I have no heirs, Charles, so to whom would I leave it all? It's become quite a sum, hasn't it?"

It seemed I had heard this preamble, or something like it, a couple of times this week. From Jean-Marie, from Edith. Leonid wasn't a spendthrift. I wondered if the same rumors that had frightened Jean-Marie had reached him. If I asked, he would say no.

None of my partners, left to himself, could be more responsible with capital than a town drunk. If I let them, they would spend Exports Méditerranée into bankruptcy. One cannot tap the same barrel forever.

"I thought a good part of your estate was in your publishing business," I said.

His head tilted down. "Erotica is not the business it used to be. East Germans have taken over. It's dangerous for an old man with brittle bones to compete with them. As for my estate, a building full of out-of-date presses is less an asset than a liability, unless a fire happens."

"Have you had a fire?"

"No. But there have been accidents among my former competitors. Editions Lyonnaise disappeared in a puff of smoke last spring. The new German equipment employs lasers, which produce an exact image. That need not matter if the subject is water lilies at Giverny, but it has become the standard in erotic publishing. Nothing may be imprecise. The voyeur is unwilling to work his imagination. Then there is the Internet. Why slink into a filthy bookstore when you can obtain a perfect digital image? We are all doomed."

"I'm sorry to hear this."

Leo raised an elaborate shrug. "It is competition, my friend. I should not complain. I will make your call now."

I waited. His business fortunes would never be as bad as he said. If he had claimed poor health, I would have been just as skeptical. For Leo, life never was better than "not *too* bad, not *terrible*." Admitting one was happy tempted the evil eye. But the years on his face and his hands bothered me. I hadn't thought before about how many of my partners were in their very late middle age, or about the implications of this for the partnership.

When he returned, he drank again to my health. There were a few drops in the bottom of our carafe, which he tipped into my glass. He hunched forward. "So, please, Charles, satisfy my curiosity. How large is my investment?"

The question was unanswerable. If I had to liquidate all the assets tomorrow, the amount received would be much less than their true value.

I shook my head. "Guiot."

"You won't tell me?"

"The number isn't in my head. What would a cement operation bring in a fire sale?"

"Or printing presses, yes. One must sell when the market is hot." He smiled faintly, unconvinced. "Guiot would like you to join him for dinner."

"Will you come along?"

"Only to introduce you."

We walked in the damp to a taxi stand. Leonid muttered and shivered inside an old leather coat. "The French grow more Russian every day. They are docile conformists. Here is more evidence. We walk on this dismal night—you should have a coat, my friend—because the French tolerate the arrogance of their taxi-driving brutes, who would pass us by in mid-block as there is an official taxi stand within one hundred meters. The customer must walk to that point in order to pay to be driven on the rest of his journey. Even Muscovites would throw rocks at the animals."

"Muscovites are the true nonconformists."

"There are fewer Communists in Moscow than in Paris," he insisted. He stopped suddenly, pointed. "There is a tribute to France's true nonconformist." A statue was scarcely visible in the mist and headlights. "Etienne Dolet, the printer of Rabelais. I feel such kinship to this man. He published *Pantagruel*, and was hanged and burned alive—both, yes—for spreading subversion. The French have never welcomed the truth."

André Guiot gave no sign of having seen me earlier. The possibility that my surveillance of him had been noted had worried me. He would have a bodyguard or two in the restaurant, and being mistaken for a stalker—in that moment before everything was set right—could be fatal.

He greeted me coolly, dismissed Leonid. Previously I have said he looked undistinguished, but that doesn't convey the full truth. If you mussed the slick white hair, let a beard grow, and dressed the man in a sleeveless undershirt, Guiot would vanish among the masses, vegetable seller or dock worker, his natural level menial. Perfectly groomed, dressed in a beautiful navy suit, he possessed the higher anonymity prized by French bureaucrats. The narrow forehead and overfull lips made him slightly ugly but not memorably so. The somewhat thick brows lent a simian look, but it is pervasive in expensive restaurants near the Bourse, the university, and the chamber of deputies, where an apelike countenance is taken as evidence of Sartrean intelligence.

"Kargman said you're a *pied-noir*."

The uncomplimentary term refers to Frenchmen of the colonial service who returned home from North Africa.

"My mother was French," I said.

"*Bicot*." Less flattering. The man was not seeking friends. He stared at me with a mild frown, as if he only now appreciated the absurdity of my presence, when normally his dinner companions were diplomats and financiers.

"Do you appreciate wines? I was thinking of the eighty-two Haut-Brion, but a fine Beaujolais might be more suitable." He raised an eyebrow, inviting me to agree.

"If you prefer Beaujolais," I said.

"It seems more suitable, I said."

He would be useful against Gardel, he and the other targets of the old man's blackmail. If he wished to insult me by ordering cheap wine, what did I care? The little game told me of the man's foolishness. If I didn't know Haut-Brion from Beaujolais, his insult would be wasted. If I knew the difference, he was needling a man who had promised help.

"The man who is causing you trouble," I said, "is a Spaniard named Carlos Gardel. His chief henchman is an Asian named Paul Chen."

"A clown."

"No, not in the least. He is a murderer. He intends to make you into an example, to encourage your friends to pay."

Guiot hoisted his chin. "He confides in you, I take it. If that is your claim, why should I trust you?"

"Gardel intends to profit from my indiscretions as well."

He didn't ask what they were, couldn't have cared.

"If we joined forces," I ventured.

"That does not appeal to me, joining forces with a *bicot*. If Gardel becomes a nuisance, we will have him deported. You, m'sieu, bring nothing to the table." But he didn't shoo me away. If he hadn't been worried, he wouldn't have let Leo introduce us. He picked at his first course. The young wine sat undisturbed in his glass. I sipped mine. He made conversation. "Kargman— how do you know the fool?"

"From business."

"What sort?" Time was, Europeans respected privacy and didn't ask. Time was. "Pornography?"

I didn't answer. To hell with him.

"Extortion?"

"Monsieur!"

"No, of course you call it something else. Your name has come up, you see, years ago, among friends of mine. The comments were not flattering. Something to do with recruiting 'partners' from among people you had something on. The view of the police, I believe, was that you were clever enough to make prosecution difficult, and cautious enough that it did not become an irresistible challenge. Not too different from this Gardel," he pointed out.

Giving up on my dinner—the squab aux pruneaux had fallen dead off a rooftop, the pinard could have come from my old sources in Algeria—I said, "The Asian won't be deported. Killing men has become an entertainment for him, in addition to business. Civilized men know the difference."

I didn't mean it as a compliment, but he nodded abruptly. Even a general who hadn't experienced the battlefield appreciated its necessity. He seemed to enjoy his soot-choked pigeon. "He is dangerous, yes, however I am well-protected."

Two young men were sitting nearby, as alert and stern as they'd been while watching over Guiot at the park that noon. They were clearly professional, but I still thought their employer was overconfident. In the park an assassin could have killed Guiot several times before the guards closed the distance.

Not expecting an answer, I said, "What leverage does Gardel have on you?"

"Very little—isn't that obvious? There is a business arrangement he threatens to expose. It is of little consequence. Do I care if *Paris Match* or *Libération* makes a fuss? Will my bank ask me to resign as a director?" Quiet sniff. "There are other banks needing capital, no? As to the physical threat, that could be made by any person against any other. It is the equivalent of the Pigalle thug's demand for my wallet. I will deal with it. Let me ask you, why do you think this extortionist chose us?"

"Politics, perhaps. You're part of the political class. Gardel believes it's time for a revolution."

"Truly?"

"He says so. From what I've seen, most of his activity isn't political." I hesitated. Certainly that was true of his takeover of Hadad's operation; and of the threats against Exports Méditerranée . But I wondered; Gardel had discerned a pattern in my business, the corrupt official class's need for financial anonymity.

"What else drives Gardel?" Guiot asked.

"He was a secret policeman in Spain, and he retains a policeman's fondness of control."

Guiot snorted. "He and his little Chinese are greedy fools."

His resources, he wanted me to know, went beyond arranging deportations. He settled back, making a show of graciousness as he ordered decent brandy, and asked me several questions about Gardel and Paul. His method was not obviously meticulous, but he covered all the ground: trying to fix Gardel's location, which I withheld, and then focusing on Paul. The Chinese was a killer, was he? Had I first-hand knowledge of a murder?

Not personally, I demurred, but his bloody reputation was well established.

"Perhaps by hearsay," Guiot said. "In the extortion business, it would be useful having friends testify that one is a hard man."

I noted the insinuation. "I have no interest in your money, General."

"Of course not." His palm warmed his brandy. "North Africans disgust me."

I handled the insult as I had the others. Only polite indifference showed on my face as I thanked Guiot for dinner. A dozen or so people, whom I did not notice at the time, told the police and the television reporters that they saw me leave the restaurant at nine forty-three, precisely. I find it unlikely they all checked their Piagets when a stranger walked out. Otherwise they were unobservant. Nobody complained publicly of desiccated squab, yet they formed a chorus, "Oh, yes, the man in the photograph, a Monsieur Mistinguett, hey? Yes, I recognize him absolutely, leaving the restaurant shortly before the other men came in, yes, a fat dark one and a tall companion, both with guns." And like that, twelve well-meaning, petty-minded French citizens convicted me without trial of having been a finger man for the assassins. It fitted, the police and prosecutors agreed, because Mistinguett was North African and so were the men with guns who knew exactly which table to visit. It took the police several days to put a name on the man so many had seen leaving General Guiot's table. By then, I had dug myself in deeper, and the name Mistinguett was synonymous with Algerian terrorism.

13

I slept soundly and phoned Cannes before noon with no suspicion that anything more had gone wrong. I had done my moral duty. I had warned André Guiot. Whatever steps he took now were his affair. If the steps happened to include removing Gardel as a nuisance to both of us, my hands would be clean. Suzy answered the phone. She said Jascha was on a mission involving Hugo. She didn't know where.

"And Aznavourian?"

"Entertaining lovers. She always does when you are away."

"Better when I'm away."

She didn't like being mocked. "We all restrain ourselves when you are here, Papa."

"Thank you."

"When you are absent, the servants respect our freedom."

"Enjoy your liberty. I'm flying into Nice this noon." It was eleven o'clock.

Apropos of nothing, she said, "Mr. Chen may stay to lunch."

In my chest I felt a stabbing jolt. I could hope I had misheard. "Who?"

"Mr. Chen. I don't, to tell you the truth, think Margaret likes him."

"And Jascha?"

"Hugo was drunk, I'll bet."

Another ear.

She went on, "So no one is keeping me prisoner, and I thought I might—"

"Hush. Where is Margaret?"

"In the boudoir, of course."

"Suzy, listen to me. Paul is working for the man who is threatening us. He amputated Hugo's ear." I didn't know whether to leave it at that or throw in Ham Hadad's head. I tried to control my panic. Paul would know that if he harmed Margaret I would come after him for his eyes, his tongue, his manhood, and only then his life. He would know, but in his present condition would the knowledge matter? Suzy hadn't said anything. I spoke. "Where are they?"

"In your office. What should I—"

"Where is Martino?" Despite his age, he could handle a knife, a fact Paul might have forgotten.

"He's with Jascha."

"Who from hotel security is on duty?"

"I don't *know* . . . one new boy was at the elevator."

Paul couldn't have placed anyone on the hotel security staff. My manager picked them himself, and he was careful. The suite wasn't under siege, I thought, except by Paul, who had walked straight in.

"How long has Paul been with Margaret?"

"I'm not sure." She stretched the last word into two syllables. Nature had not made her a serious person, and events that demanded seriousness were, to her sweetly self-centered mind, unfair. "It could be half an hour?"

"Where are you?"

"Next door, in the library."

"Are they arguing?"

"Not loudly. She treats most men coolly. Haven't you noticed?"

It was overexposure to them in her youth, I thought; couldn't see that it mattered now. If Paul had lost all semblance of reason, Margaret wouldn't be able to restrain him with scorn.

"Don't go to the door," I said. "Buzz the office and tell Margaret that chef wants her lunch order, and should it be for one or two? I'll wait. Don't hang up. Can you manage?"

I listened. When she picked up the handset in less than a minute, I'd heard enough. Two for lunch. "When she answered," I said, "was she on the speaker phone?"

"How did you know?"

He would want to hear.

As much as I wanted to talk to Margaret, I didn't dare. I might be able to control my words but not the tone. If Paul heard fear, he would know he and the Spaniard had been betrayed.

"Suzy, dear, have you seen Ali's boat in the harbor in the last few days?"

"I don't know."

"Any of the crew?"

Several of them were young and handsome.

"Oh, yes, Philippe was ashore this morning. He plans to become—"

"Never mind. In a moment I want you to go down to the Corniche and hitch a ride to Ali's yacht. I'll try to reach him. In case I don't, tell him the family is in jeopardy and I'm entrusting you to his care. His and Philippe's. That should make you happy."

"He's not at all mature."

"Hang up now, get going. I'll come out to the boat this evening."

Alerting Ali could wait. I phoned the hotel again, found my reliable manager on duty. He picked up an extension in the kitchen and turned on the practiced affability. "What is your pleasure, Monsieur Charles?"

What is my pleasure? Send in the maniacs. Summon Mademoiselle Aznavourian, presto. Lend Jascha a long rifle. I'd had only seconds to decide.

"I want you to set fire to the room directly under my office."

After an indrawn breath he was silent.

As an afterthought, I said, "Try not to disturb the other guests."

"I was a perfect gentleman. You overreacted."

Paul speaking. Margaret had said he was calm. A killing took the manic edge off, like a bishop's trip to the boys' choir. So he had come to visit, he said, assuming I had returned the previous night, and had remained and chatted with my charming assistant about Rive Gauche restaurants only to demonstrate, at Carlos Gardel's behest, the extent of our vulnerability.

"But the old fiend is quite happy with you right now," Paul said. "I told him you had led us to Guiot. He's in a rare mood."

My expression must have been rewarding. This was my first hint of Guiot's fate, which had come too late for the morning editions. I had noticed that security at the airport seemed to have been tightened, but my papers identified me as a French national and the suspicion of anyone with Algerian roots had yet to take hold.

"I didn't lead you to Guiot."

I was sure of it.

"Hey, I suppose it's possible Munifal was tailing the general. But he won't say anything that gets you off the hook."

"Tell me what happened."

"All I know is what I see on television. They're saying this gentleman was gunned down at dinner last night. Eight or ten torso shots. Pfut, pfut, pfut, pfut, pfut. Then there were those two dudes at another table who got in on the act. Bodyguards, not good ones. Helluva show, according to my guys. By the way, we waited till you were out of the place."

"Thank you."

"So now you've only got to play ball with the old bastard. I'll be there to help."

He was starting to jump again. I left him at the table and walked into the hotel. The fire had been a little more distracting than I'd intended. Two people from the maintenance staff had filled a metal waste can with shredded paper and set it ablaze, while two others fanned smoke onto the balcony. A couple of oily rags helped the cause. The scheme worked well until the fire climbed the lower room's curtains. When the men rushed in a hose, that room and two beneath were damaged by water. One guest fled threatening legal revenge. Margaret had walked out uninjured. That was the main thing.

I had a stiff drink at the bar and took to the stairs. The young man from hotel security did everything but snap a salute. Good boy. Keep the collar pressed and the shoes bright and nobody would blame him for the psychopaths who slip past.

Margaret had packed several mismatched suitcases. She was wearing slacks and a blazer, a bright scarf on her hair and white canvas shoes.

"Have you packed Suzy's things?"

"Only my own." Her glance stopped short of me. "I had hoped to be gone when you returned, to avoid anything unpleasant."

It's true that I didn't understand her. How could one? I threw myself onto the couch. "What is unpleasant? You are safe. Suzy is safe. Jascha I will kill, but—" I shrugged. So what?

"The way you talk so casually about killing, I find that unpleasant." Her mouth was prim, a condition I'd never noticed before. "All right. I feel bad about abandoning you—now, especially. But you are too much like the others—the Gardels, the Paul Chens. You are ruthless."

I am, in fact, the opposite of ruthless.

"There is no way," I said patiently, "that the fire could have gotten out of control. The men had a hose from the stairwell before they struck a match." Untrue, but they should have done.

"I am not talking about that. Paul was extremely candid. He is very high on you."

The little shit!

"So is Gardel," I said calmly.

"So you buy your safety with another man's life." This, from a woman who a few days earlier made it my life or Gardel's.

"Yes, of course," I said. "I led the apes to Guiot and held their coats. No, I reloaded their guns! There are two things wrong with that. If you were thinking with your head rather than your *connasse*, I wouldn't have to explain."

Her face was white. "You needn't anyway."

"But it's a pleasure. On the most rudimentary level, there is the fact Paul didn't need a bird dog to point out the general. He had Guiot under surveillance before I arrived in Paris. His men followed Guiot to our rendezvous. Second, if I had traded them the general for our safety, I wouldn't have been panicked by Paul's visit." Untrue, too. The logic was all right, but my knowledge of Paul would have swept away logic. There would be no reason to hurt her, but did he need a reason? I added, "I didn't know what happened to Guiot until Paul told me"—convincing watch inspection—"twenty minutes ago."

She was silent.

"I did my best to warn André Guiot. That was, I'll concede, self-serving. I wanted Guiot and his friends to align themselves with me against Gardel." I sighed. "I am sorry he is dead. He seemed an unassuming man."

Margaret sat at the desk. "I believe that you did not assist in the murder. But I am not certain it matters."

I was tired, emptied of the fear that had held me for hours. I was too tired to admit the truth: how willingly I would burn down the hotel to keep her safe. "No, it probably doesn't matter," I said. "Your emotions rule you. How could facts matter?"

"So it is either emotions or the *connasse*," she said. "Perhaps your next assistant will be coldly rational enough to suit you."

"You can't leave."

"No?"

"Suzy and Jascha are still in danger."

"Nonsense. Gardel adores you, you said so yourself."

"Guiot's associates won't adore me. That will suit Paul and Gardel, whom I will need as allies."

"You have really created a mess for yourself."

That seemed unfair. The mess was not of my making. But her tone was softer, and she had decided she could bear to look at me again. So I hung my head and said, "The mess is hardest on others."

"Oh, yes," she said, then broke into laughter. "You say that so well! As convincing as when you tell Edith she must not live beyond her means. So if I must not leave you, what shall I do?"

In fact, it was obvious she had to go. She knew nothing of guns or knives. I needed people around me who did. "I want you to join Ali's entourage. Take your computer. I need the names of Guiot's fellow crooks, so I can plead my innocence to them. And I'm afraid Gardel won't remain satisfied with our status."

"What will he do?"

"Demand some new show of loyalty. I don't know. Perhaps arrange for the general's friends to find me. Photographs of one of them shooting me would be more useful to a blackmailer than an old scandal from Africa."

Two maintenance men entered timidly and began rolling up carpets. The office had escaped both smoke and water, but the smell of burned fabric from the room below clung to everything.

I used the phone on my desk and reached Ali, who immediately thanked me for sending such a lovely gift. "I believe I've fallen in love again. My first wife was seventeen, you know."

"You have my permission if you have hers," I said. Ali was close to seventy, with a backward ruff of jet-black dyed hair, smoker's wrinkles, a forty-six-inch waist, and toothpick legs that lifted the round torso and neckless head to an improbable height of nearly six feet. But he had his charms. He told good stories and had lived as if tomorrow were his last day for as long as I had known him. When Ali Souidan was in his forties, he had owned the tankers that brought in Algerian plonk wine disguised as Liberian crude, and our business relationship had been happy and profitable. He spent money on women as if each was the last he would have. Suddenly worried, I added, "Her brother Jascha, on the other hand, would kill you."

He laughed. "Then I would be a legend in death as I've been in life. Your daughter is safe with me, old friend. As you know."

"I know. I would like to entrust Margaret to you as well."

"Temptations, temptations. Are things that dangerous for you ashore?"

"They're difficult."

"You should live at sea, Charles. Problems vanish. I'll send a boat to the basin. Half an hour?"

"An hour." However tentative our reconciliation, it needed to be consummated. We went to bed quickly, leaving the window open to the garden. My questions yielded little. What had Paul wanted? "Only to assure me of his friendship for you," she said. "And of Captain Gardel's good intentions from now on. It was like being purred at by a snake." I knew how she felt. He had wrapped himself around my leg as well. I walked Margaret down to the basin only a few minutes late for the boat.

The pilot was one of Ali's sons, middle-aged and sour, as stalky as the old man. "Papa says we may go to Corsica for a few days," he said as we loaded suitcases aboard. The launch was the classic sort that might have decorated Lake Como forty years ago, when Ali was a poor immigrant, with deeply varnished decks and shining chrome horns at the bow. They sped away on heavy twin outboards, and I thought of how peaceful Corsica sounded with only a few separatists planting bombs or machine-gunning soldiers.

I went back to the hotel. A hundred Euros soothed the concerns of a municipal official who had heard a fire bomb might have been thrown. We inspected the lower room together and agreed the fire had been electrical as a result of a guest's negligence. The fool had been a drunken German, I explained, who twice had spilled garlic schnapps on the television. He had run off without paying the bill or making good on the damages.

Jascha returned with Hugo at midafternoon. Two of the clod's fingers had been broken before he agreed to call and plead for help. Jascha found him three hours later in an abandoned farmhouse, bound and bored. I sent Hugo down to his grandfather to have the fingers taped and asked Jascha, "What were you planning to do if the gang was there?"

"I assumed they would be nearby, to ambush me." He opened his jacket and unslung a rifle with a short stock and a mounted scope. He gave me a sheepish look, as though expecting to be slapped.

"Your marksmanship is not good enough for this," I said. "Did Margaret know?"

"Certainly not this. It didn't occur to either of us that Paul was trying to lure me off the nest. You said he was in Paris."

"Why didn't you run your plan past me?"

"I should have. But you were in Paris—"

"And you saw a chance to be a hero. Or to draw blood. Which was it?"

"In truth, both." He threw his jacket on top of the rifle. "So you set fire to the hotel? I was only hoping to shoot people."

I ignored his insolence. I wouldn't have let him go to Hugo's assistance, if he'd asked, because he was worth infinitely more to me than Martino's grandson. He wasn't that sentimental about his own skin.

"So how are things?" he said.

I told him the truth. "If the police can identify me, I'll be arrested for Guiot's murder. I was in the restaurant with him. I was lurking near his office. I followed him to a meeting with someone who works at Élysée Palace."

"How do you know where he works?"

"I don't actually. I saw him go into the palace; he appeared to be returning from lunch. We will try to find out who he is."

Jascha went to shower. I sat at the desk and phoned Leonid

Kargman. He was untalkative, not ready to imply I had tricked him but burdened by the possibility. Or possibilities. If I had tricked him into setting up André Guiot, then the implications for his investment were grim. He cared more about the nestegg than about one French general.

"I'm going on holiday, Charles," he said. "Perhaps Lisbon."

"Do you need money?"

"Not just now. Tell me straight. If I retired, would there be enough to keep an old man alive?"

I said yes and he said "Good, good," as if reassured, and I said good as if I thought we agreed, which I suppose is a fair way to describe mutual distrust. Then I explained that the assassins had followed Guiot and could have killed him anywhere but chose a setting to implicate me.

"That is most unfortunate."

"It puts me at their mercy."

"Yes, I see." The old voice betrayed his real feelings. There was nothing I could do to convince Leo of my innocence. So my purpose in calling was thwarted. If he knew anything of Guiot's associates, he wouldn't tell me.

He knew something of their character. He hadn't taken a holiday in all the years I'd known him.

My options were limited. Most involved preemptive violence against either Gardel or Guiot's friends. Violence or compliant surrender. There is a tradition in my father's world of turning one's neck to the knife. Allah wills. The tradition hadn't served my father well.

It's a matter of record — inconvenient to those now defaming me — that I sought the nonviolent course.

Waiting for Michael Weeks to return my call, I went downstairs. Earlier I had brushed off my manager's complaints about the tax examiners. Now I found Robert justifying the most trivial invoices. His interrogators were the overweight blond woman I'd seen with Laval and a man operating a tiny computer. Both ignored me.

When he caught sight of me, Robert jumped up and came

out of the office. His face was red and damp. "Sheer harassment! Next the old trout will want to see how many drinks we comp you at the bar."

"Is she focusing on me?"

"I tried to tell you. Anything involving Mistinguett they insist on seeing—book entries, original receipts. It is difficult."

As many of those records never existed, "difficult" was a nice description.

"The rent, for example," Robert said.

"What have you told them?"

"Only that I'm certain those records will turn up."

"We can't insert a rent payment into the monthly postings—it would throw off all the totals."

He shrugged. "We could delete something else. But they have been through three years of monthly postings—and weekly and daily accounts—and the absence of rent payments by you has been noticed. They have not gone back ten years, however, and there might have been a one-time payment then. It may be a couple of days before they get that far, unless I lead them."

"Are they finding any other problems?"

"No."

"Let them lead themselves then." The last thing I wanted was to free up two bureaucrats whose curiosity could cause me nothing but trouble. As matters stood, Laval might be building a stinky little tax case.

He wouldn't be limiting himself for long. The murder of the deskbound hero of the Fifth Republic would invigorate him once my name was attached.

"Are they still taking meals at the hotel?"

"She does. Bourride every day."

"Have chef spill pepper into her supper."

He went back to the deadening chore of matching invoices with ledger entries, and I went into the bar for a cup of Africanized coffee and tried Michael Weeks's office. This time he answered.

"Is this urgent, Charles?"

"It's possible I will be arrested in a few days." Sooner if Guiot had told the maître d' he was expecting a Monsieur Mistinguett. My stomach was acid. I asked the barman for a bottle of Badoit.

"What have you gone and done, old man?"

It took twenty minutes to describe the events, correct his misinterpretations, and overrule his suggestions. His best proposal was that I join Ali's crew and spend a few months at sea. "Throwing yourself on the mercy of a cop like Laval—you may as well supply the hangman his rope."

"I'm not seeking mercy. I want you to make a straightforward approach to Laval and his commanders. Tell them your client has important information, feels it his duty to share the information, and wants assurances that the police will not make unreasonable assumptions."

"Or reasonable ones?"

"Do you have contacts at the Justice Ministry or not?"

"I have contacts. The risk is that Laval has a grudge and only your balls will satisfy him."

"There's no reason for a grudge."

"You helped Chen get away with murder."

"Paul hadn't killed anyone that time."

"And the way you used to advertise that you'd done Yves Bulant, that wouldn't stick in a policeman's craw, would it?"

"It was only advertising."

"And when Eric Laval pays a call, you don't mock him as a cretin?" He clucked. "No, you're right, Charlie. There's no reason for the police to have a grudge against you."

"They can feel however they like," I said. "I just want an understanding. If I give them a master criminal—Carlos Gardel—I want to be left alone in return."

"I'll make the offer," he said.

14

I drove up to the villa alone. The summons had been for six-thirty. A bodyguard I had seen before showed me past an iron gate into a garden. Dusk wasn't imminent. Sunlight angling between closely spaced pine trees lay on the heads of the tallest flowers. The layered light created an impression that evening rose from the grass like ivy tendrils and had climbed to about my waist. Chrysanthemums bloomed profusely in urns at either end of the little park. The largest urns stood atop a low western wall in front of the pines. The north and south sides were bordered by hedges, along which ran gravel paths that defined the square and then quartered it. Gardel was at the farthest corner, walking slowly but without assistance. He wore a black suit, a collarless striped shirt, and a white shawl over his shoulders. The sunlight that reached his head found only yellowed tints of white as if bone were visible through the scalp. The head dipped as he walked. Old spider, looking for careless birds.

"You must be proud of your son," he said when we came close. "He has the heart of a bullfighter. This morning, Paul's men could easily have killed him, but I could not bear it. As a young man, I was like your boy. Nothing frightened me. Nothing stood in my way. The youngest girls adored me as a hero, and I deflowered a hundred of them. If politics hadn't consumed me, I might have been a great lover. But I found my calling elsewhere."

He had found it in the execution squads, Stalin's and Franco's. The calling mattered, not its sponsor.

I was silent. My distaste for him couldn't be hidden entirely.

"I still possess the courage to act boldly," the old man said. With the sun behind his head, I could make out little of the sunken face. I heard the crackle of his laugh again without having seen the lips move. It wasn't the sound of dry sticks snapping, I realized, but of little birds' bones. I would have been only partly surprised to see the sunlight illuminating giant webs spun between the flower urns, webs full of feathers.

Someone who had been in a Spanish prison had written that he pictured Death as a Spaniard. I understood.

I am not attempting to dehumanize Gardel. He was not—is not—a spider but an old man, possessing the attributes of humanity: self-awareness, a habit of walking upright, a memory of wrongs that must be avenged. There is more to a man than that, and there was more to Gardel—memories of family, friends, lovers, though I doubt in the sense those terms are normally used. He boasted of having the courage to move boldly. A spider moves boldly in leaping from cover to enshroud a moth. The kill requires no courage, only knowledge of the weakness of the moth.

"I considered letting Paul have his way," Gardel said. "You did not, strictly speaking, obey me. But I knew that if Paul's men eliminated the boy, it would not be possible for you and I to work together. The same was true for Mademoiselle Aznavourian. You would make some futile vow of revenge."

He fell silent, from lack of breath or so I could say something futile. A flash came through the trees as the sun fell below the hill, and the garden became cooler. The silence seemed inevitable. The phenomenon occurs on the liveliest streets of the

Côte. Dusk arrives and everyone takes a breath—There, it's done!—before launching into the evening rituals.

The dry voice suddenly wanted to hurry. "Then I would be distracted by you, instead of having my fun. That is all I enjoy now, making *l'aristocratie politique* pay for their criminal arrogance. It entertains me. You may go now."

"I thought you wanted to discuss something."

"No. I wanted to assure myself you would come when summoned."

He hobbled toward me, and I stepped aside so he could pass. He went ahead. From the back, seeing only the pale head and the shawl and the hunched black clothing, he could have been a village priest, or an undertaker. I saw the bodyguard waiting at the gate. I stood in the deepening gloom as Gardel's feet crunched away on the path. When he reached the garden's center, the guard came and lent his arm. They crept toward the gate, and I walked back and looked at the flowers. From a corner of the wall, it was possible to look down the slope beyond the trees, past steep cliffs, and see miles away the distant shimmering Mediterranean. There were a couple of dozen places along the road where a sudden precipice or double-back opened a vista like this. The Saracens and Romans would have thrown inconvenient people off those cliffs. So would Germans and armies of local cutthroats. The cliffs remained useful places for automobile crashes.

Gardel had warned me, if I looked at it that way. Tonight's ride down from the hills could be dangerous. Paul had lured my son to a rendezvous he wanted to make lethal. Gardel had lured me . . . because he wanted to know I would come. Perhaps.

Or because he had decided I could never be trusted.

If it was Paul, he would prefer to use a knife.

I walked out of the garden and didn't see the old man or the guard. If he had decided I couldn't be trusted, what had tipped his decision? There hadn't been time for Michael Weeks to approach the Ministry of Justice, or for anyone there to have warned Gardel.

Leonid Kargman? That old friend thought I was on Gardel's side.

Michael Weeks, informing Gardel directly? A client never knew where he fit among Michael's priorities. If Gardel had started his research with the lawyer, it would explain his knowing so much about me. Possible. I couldn't dismiss the thought. It was more likely, however, that Gardel had learned about me by collecting buttons—a few from Paul, more from Jean-Marie, and details of our current household from a spy in the hotel.

There was no sign of Paul in the courtyard.

I walked to the car, bearing only an abstract fear of the invisible rifle and night scope. I could see that the back seat was empty. I got in, drove out of the compound with the headlights on high beam. The evening traffic down to the coast was heavy. I pulled off the highway as soon as I could. Parked on a side road, I watched the traffic. After a while I turned on the radio. Its faint light fell on the floor. I noticed a corner of the package lying under the passenger's seat.

Boom.

It was the size of a large magazine, a reinforced brown envelope. There was no writing on the front. I lifted the lightly stuck flap. Photographs. Now I switched on the dome light. Large, matte-finished shots were awkwardly composed, as if taken discreetly. They showed two men having dinner and conversation in a restaurant. Their faces were mostly in profile or three-quarter views, easily recognized. The middle-aged man on the left had strong Mediterranean features and intelligent eyes. He was handsome. He appeared in the first photograph to be listening to a man whose head was narrow at the top and whose lips were heavy, a man who wore the arrogance of *l'aristocrate politique* as comfortably as his fine suit. In the second photo, the Mediterranean man was gesturing broadly. In the third his face was frozen in anger. The fourth and fifth shots appeared to capture a single look of scorn on the political man's face. Sixth, seventh, eighth. The Mediterranean man rises, departs, a man in a topcoat appears, seen only from the shoulders down. The remaining diner's arrogant face displays shock. Ninth, tenth, et cet. A fat man in a trench coat joins them, his back to the camera, a weapon in a fat hand, puffs of smoke, carnage. Chaos.

Curious fact. I hadn't noticed wearing the expressions of distaste, anger and contempt that I saw in the photographs. Here was objective proof that I was not so good at keeping thoughts to myself.

Fifteen prints in all. I slid them into the envelope. If Gardel suspected me of betraying him, the photographs would find their way to a prosecutor. They could support a case that I had set up André Guiot for the men who killed him.

I started the car and drove back to Cannes. The pictures were damning, yes, but I could see them working in my favor. It wouldn't help a murder prosecution that I had copies of the same incriminating pictures as did the prosecutor. An innocent photographer would hardly supply copies to both the authorities and the assassins.

The contradiction was obvious, but in the end would it matter? The evidence that I had been with Guiot in his last few minutes was irrefutable. A close examination of the final frames might disclose that time had elapsed between my departure and Guiot's death. My table setting might have been cleared. A better bottle might have appeared. I didn't bother to look.

I phoned Michael Weeks to check his progress, but there was no answer.

I arrived at the hotel expecting to find Laval waiting for me with a black van. The lobby was bustling with our prosperous clientele. There was not—as Michael would say—a copper in sight.

Jascha found the bomb. He set a cardboard box on my desk the next morning, in front of my juice, and lifted the flaps so I could admire the construction.

"It has a rocker, you see? One sharp curve on the road, or a bump, and the contacts on either side close the circuit. The battery leads were connected here." *Here* was an oily, misshapen block of green clay.

"Where did you find it?"

"In your car. It wasn't there last night or you would be in pieces. This is domestic product, Papa. It's what the *piscine* used to sink the Greenpeace boat in New Zealand. I would say General Guiot's friends are angry with you."

"And with Gardel, I hope."

"If they know about him. You said Guiot had only met Paul. The Spaniard has set things up so that you appear to be Paul's boss."

Guiot's friends had responded quickly. Less than thirty-six hours had elapsed since Guiot's murder.

"Take the damned thing away."

"And the plastique?"

I didn't want it in our rooms, where the police might search. I had no use for the stuff, no plans for taping a few kilos to Gardel's ass. Guiot's friends I couldn't blame; they had acted, perhaps too hastily, on misinformation. But the murderous Basque had disrupted my life enough.

"Throw it to the fish," I said. "Somewhere the tide won't bring it back."

"They will have more."

"I know."

I finished breakfast, talked by telephone with Margaret. They had gotten no farther than Cassis. Ali had received invitations to a nude swimming party at a notorious Belgian's chateau.

"I had to threaten reprisals," Margaret said, "to keep your daughter from going."

"What sort of reprisals?"

"There are things women know about each other."

"Is that what prevented you from going?"

"Swimming naked with Ali Souidan prevented me."

Ali would regard a minor indulgence like that as his due. Having been denied, he would be out of sorts.

I said, "Are you in port?"

"No, at anchor. Ali is taking precautions for us."

"Where is Suzy?"

"Sunning on the top deck. There is a crewman she has an eye on."

"Bad luck for the dago back home."

"What do you expect of her?"

Obedience? Good sense? No point in asking for either.

"I have two names," she went on. "Pascal Pourquery and Georges Blasco. Both generals. Both served in the Central African Republic at the same time as Guiot. Blasco didn't have such a high rank then. He was attached to the embassy. Pourquery seems to have been an adviser to President Giscard. I didn't realize we had installed a series of dictators there." By "we" she meant France.

"Where did you think they came from?"

"I thought they grew naturally, like cocoa nuts."

"What else?"

"Both men live in Paris. Georges Blasco is a businessman. Pascal Pourquery, who is from an aristocratic family, directs security at the President's palace."

And struts, I thought.

"You've done very well," I said. "What about pictures?"

"General Blasco was in *L'Express* six years ago when he bought a soap factory in Marseilles. I will send you the photo. Security people are shy, but I will try to find something on Pourquery."

"I have probably seen him." Tall, his hair still blondish though he had to be in his sixties, trim mustache, determined walk. Guiot had met Pascal Pourquery in the park. I wondered if Paul Chen had any idea of how well-connected a man he had murdered. I said into the handset, and I didn't know whose ears, "I will have to make them understand that Gardel is the enemy, that I am an innocent bystander, a victim just as André Guiot was."

Bit flowery.

"Yes, you will," Margaret said.

As soon as I put down the phone I regretted having kept the conversation on business. Out of habit, I assumed with Margaret that the important things between intimate people need not be said. Those things are either felt or not. How many times had I pledged devotion to my first wife? In the end, I was no more loyal than she.

A more substantial regret was having elicited the boat's approximate position off Cassis.

My phone clicked, and I inspected the page she had gleaned from an old article on Georges Blasco's business triumphs. The photograph was adequate. A jowly man with thick hair dropping close to hairless brows, a square face and tiny mouth. He looked more like a sergeant than a general.

Pourquery and Blasco. Blasco and Pourquery. The speed with which the bomb had appeared told me we weren't going to negotiate. I could assume two other unpleasant facts as well. The generals knew I had dined with Guiot, even if the police hadn't identified me yet. And Pourquery had sent security forces to murder me. The last conclusion was inescapable. I couldn't imagine a general traveling down from Paris with plastique in his suitcase, identifying and locating my car and placing the charge, all by himself in one night. The operation required an organization.

France is deeply politicized. That Pourquery would deploy the palace guard on a private mission was barely shocking. To the *aristocrate politique* at risk, the mission would be a matter of state.

I told myself not to overreact. Another explanation was possible. Gardel might have had the bomb planted . . . but no, he had had ample opportunity to dispense with my services last night. Instead, he had shown me pictures, which bound me to him.

Not Gardel. It might even be a mistake to assume Gardel was still alive. Pourquery seemed determined to settle matters fast.

It took me ten minutes in the office to put together the

necessities, while Jascha packed our bags. There were more things than one might think. A certain amount of cash in several currencies, financial records on memory sticks, an oversexed portable computer with satellite capability. Telephone. A small Czech automatic pistol. Jascha would have an array of his own toys. Two telephone calls. One arranged lunch with people I had no intention of meeting. The other was to housekeeping. When a maid arrived with the laundry cart, Jascha took over as she waited in the hall. We loaded our luggage into the cart and piled bedding on top. Jascha trundled the cart into the hall. "Take this load down to Martino's room," he told the maid. "He's not expecting it. If he makes a fuss, tell him I'll be along in five minutes to break his fingers." She liked that. Jascha could have said anything and she would have liked it. She was fifty years old, with oily cheeks and a romantic heart.

We descended the fire stairs with the stealth of rent-beaters. Through the mesh-covered window I could see the main registration desk and, to the left, the door to Robert's office. A little after ten in the morning, the area was busy. I couldn't see the tax frau or her assistant.

"If she sees us, she sees us," Jascha said.

He stepped out and headed for the rear gardens. I waited a few seconds, then emerged with a hand on the gun in my pocket.

I never tour the hotel with the air of an owner on inspection. Indeed, only my reliable manager knows that Mistinguett and the company that owns the Métropole are interchangeable. Even that is not accurate. If the diligent sow from the revenue office ever traced the hotel's ownership as far as Exports Méditerranée , she would reach a dead end. Exports Méditerranée S.A. was a French corporation that paid French taxes on its income. Its sole stockholder was a partnership also calling itself Exports Méditerranée , which was registered in Switzerland. The sole partner of the partnership was a corporation—Exports Méditerranée, of course—domiciled in Vaduz. The Liechtenstein corporation's only stockholder was a partnership based in the

Caymans. If anyone ever penetrated the barriers of Cayman secrecy, ownership would trace to an obscure—and seemingly empty—subsidiary of a French corporation called Exports Méditerranée S.A. The circularity of it all, having Exports owned by one of its properties, amused me. I could imagine an exhausted bureaucrat, having trekked through the desert among hollow corporate bones for months and finding himself (or herself) back at my office, throwing up hands and crying, "Yes, but who *owns* it?" That would be a most interesting question, as no owners are recorded, certainly none of my shy and retiring partners. The important question is who controls it, and the answer—fortunately for all concerned—is Mistinguett.

The front door was no more than twenty feet from the registration desk. I walked out drawing only a passing glance from one clerk. It was a fine weekend morning, sunny and cool. I walked directly to the municipal garage a block north. The time for subterfuge would come later.

A second bomb seemed unlikely so soon, but I inspected the Lancia with care. When I drove up at the hotel's back gate, Martino was waiting. The old man opened the rear door, and Jascha strongarmed a reluctant Hugo into the back seat. Martino fetched the laundry cart as I popped the trunk. As far as I could tell, we were never under observation.

We caught the slow traffic toward La Napoule. I made phone calls while Jascha drove. Martino dozed in the back seat, beside Hugo, who sulked. We had had to bring the old man's grandson. When Hugo was vulnerable, so was Martino. Jascha chafed at the logic. "He will be worse than useless," he complained, "unless he's drunk and asleep."

At the D4, we turned north and I finally connected with Ali Souidan. I told him we had had further trouble and the risk to Margaret and Suzy had risen.

"Then so has the risk to me," he observed. "Thank you for the warning. I shall put them ashore."

While I clenched my teeth, he laughed uproariously.

"Do you trust your crew enough to arm them?"

Suddenly he was sober. "They would not be my crew otherwise."

"My phone calls from the hotel may have been intercepted, in which case your boat is known. I don't want to know your plans," I said, "but please act accordingly."

"Of course. And where are you, Charles?"

"En route to San Raphael." It was a chi-chi resort farther down the coast—opposite our present direction. My true destination was a far smaller, secluded place. I added another tasty detail: "I'm meeting two journalists from *L'Express*. It's time that certain facts were exposed."

"Ooh, exciting! No wonder you have enemies."

"I'm nobody's enemy by choice," I said. "But when people who misunderstand attempt to kill me, what can I do?"

He seemed bored by such self-serving palaver. "If they kill you, Charles, may I keep the women?"

I disconnected. We were climbing now, well above the coastal plain on a modern highway that happened to be lightly traveled. I had picked up nothing suspicious behind us. Jascha flicked a glance at me. "There is a van a kilometer ahead. He made the turn just before we did. He has speeded up—you see on the curve, the dark van? He knows we have nowhere to go for a while. About a hundred meters back, the blue Mercedes has closed up a bit. When I let the speed drop, he keeps his steady. It would look suspicious if he maintained distance. He was much farther back when we left Cannes."

I used the mirrors to inspect the dozen vehicles behind us, strung out on the long slope. Apart from the van, only a handful of cars was visible ahead, all at a considerable distance. I trusted Jascha's read on the ones to be worried about. Whether they were the generals' people or Gardel's was another matter. In any case, they would be in communication with their masters. In a half-hour, anything on the road could be an enemy.

The palm trees and flowers of the coast had been replaced by pines and brown fields. The air had cooled, and Jascha had switched on the heater after Hugo complained. We went on another two minutes. No change in the problem vehicles' positions. Hugo announced he was car sick. Jascha didn't slow or look around. "If you puke in the car," he said, "I'll amputate your last ear."

"I'm really sick. I can't help it." The idiot looked terrible, white and damp, hands clamped to his mouth, the bandaged temple and other wounds bloodless. Between his fingers he was hyperventilating. His face leaned toward Jascha's neck.

"*Ferme la bouche!*"

Jascha cut across the right lane and skidded onto the shoulder. Before we had stopped, I had the Czech BRNO in my hand. We both got out on the passenger side. The blue Mercedes was our concern. From a hundred meters back, the driver had had no chance to react. The car swept past two lanes away. No flicker of brake lights. That was good. Then I glimpsed three male heads, all turning to look at us. A natural reaction when the quarry has done the unexpected. The tail wagged once, as if the driver had checked an impulse to head for the shoulder. Jascha held a small Galil by the barrel.

We were in the wide open, with no buildings in sight. The position was impossible to defend, but for the same reason not particularly easy to attack. A shootout would be bad for both sides.

We watched the oncoming traffic while Hugo vomited into the grass.

None of the faces that blurred past seemed to pay us much attention. Our weapons were concealed by the open doors. The wind rocked us. In the silence as we waited for the next wave of traffic, Hugo groaned and gagged. Straightening, he wobbled back and forth along the shoulder. Kicking dirt over the mess, Martino said, "I apologize, patron. I didn't know he was so weak and useless."

Jascha withdrew a two-liter can of water from the trunk, handed it to Martino. "Tell him to wash himself off. I don't want the car smelling of puke."

He came over to me. "We have a long drive ahead, boss, and

they'll be waiting for us. They will assume we're armed and act accordingly."

Which could mean anything: a machine-gun ambush, an overladen truck, a rocket.

"You're fond of imagining disasters," I said.

"I'm fond of avoiding them, which requires thinking ahead. What do you suggest we do?"

The immediate options were limited. The Mercedes had taken to the shoulder near the crest of the hill. A stationary rear window reflected light down the hillside. We could cross the grassy median and head back toward the coast. But the maneuver would be seen, and any trailing vehicles would be alerted.

"We'll drive on," I said.

My first destination no longer appealed. A small, self-contained resort made a bad hiding place, a hopeless fortress. Men with Pourquery's connections might deploy substantial resources. Discovery by a concerted search would be only a day or two away.

"Back in the car, then." As Hugo passed, Jascha grabbed him and sniffed. "You smell like a whore's asshole. Run along behind us."

The boy jerked free and scrambled into the back seat.

"Straight ahead," I said, "at speed."

He pushed the Lancia uphill and had covered half the distance to the waiting car in less than a minute. Two men were making a point of not hurrying as they returned to the vehicle. They hadn't stopped for any particular reason. The binoculars hanging from the neck of a totally bald man were for birding. The Lancia had topped 130 kph. If they opened fire, we would be a difficult target.

In the long haul, we couldn't outrun the Mercedes. It had more speed, more mass, more range. They knew that.

We were closing on them.

"The driver's door," I said.

Swerving from the travel lane, we reached the paved

shoulder a dozen meters behind the Mercedes. The driver's door was closing, too slowly. On the impact, the Lancia tried to dive to the right as Jascha steered left. We were veering across two traffic lanes as I watched the loose Mercedes door cartwheeling behind us. Had the driver let go in time?

Jascha regained control.

"They will radio ahead," he said.

"Slow down and find your way to the outside lane."

The drivers behind us who had witnessed our stunt against the Mercedes were steering wide. I had been listening for the whine of crumpled metal against rubber, waiting for our right front tire to explode. We passed the summit and pulled onto the median verge. I got out and checked our damage. We had an ugly fender, an empty headlight socket, but the tire had clearance.

The chances were good that they had lost sight of us. Across the grassy center strip, heavy traffic hurtled south, mostly caravans of refrigerated trucks descending to the coast. We drove across the median, accelerated into a gap in the traffic. Jascha edged right, and we passed the disabled Mercedes screened by a truck.

A minute later I watched several police cars rushing north. It shouldn't have been surprising after a road accident, but the speed of the response was ominous. A corrupt political class taints the civil service.

We took the next exit onto a two-lane road that meandered on a northeasterly bias. There was no traffic. After ten minutes, we hid on a farm track and waited for any chase cars to pass. None did.

I tried phoning Michael Weeks's office, knowing it was futile on a Saturday, and his machine answered. I couldn't think of a suitably foul message to leave. I tried his home and got no answer.

Forty minutes later we entered a village made up of a dozen old brick and stone buildings. It was situated on a hillside on the way to nowhere. The stone walls were fortified, and the leaning brick structures dated from some time after the Saracens' visits waned. When no one has pillaged for a while, it's tempting to put out awnings and tables. Jascha nosed the sedan in beside other cars on the approach to an open-air restaurant. He and Martino got out, leaving me with Hugo, who was snoring. I tried phoning the lawyer.

There was little he could do, I told myself.

A second-deputy in the Ministry of Justice wouldn't send the CRS smashing down Villa Balzar's door merely because Michael Weeks, Esq. had spun a fantastic story. And nothing would convince Blasco or Pourquery of my innocence if they preferred to believe otherwise.

Too much to hope that the old torturer and the generals would be mutually cancelling threats.

It was too late to rely on Michael. Too late to talk about getting my affairs in order.

As I got out of the car, the phone rang. Not many people knew the number. To my answer, a familiar voice said, "You held out on me," Inspector Laval said. "You failed to mention that Hamilton Hadad has left the business, and the world."

"I was unaware of either fact.'

"Ah, there's an image. Mistinguett pretending to be an ostrich." Laval chuckled in self-appreciation. "And still you are so uncurious. You haven't asked if by 'leaving the world' I mean what you think I do. You haven't asked what happened to him. Personally, I would have expected to find Hadad strangled in some homoerotic tryst. Instead, we have the corpse in a ditch, missing its sweet smile and moist eyes. It took us half a day to find the head, monsieur. There are dogs in the area, you know."

"What area is that?"

"I'll play your game. It was on the N85, near Mougins. Really not that far from Cannes. Where are you now, m'sieu? I'm at the hotel, and you're not here."

Could Laval hope to trace my location through this call? I broke the connection, switched off the phone. Jascha and Martino had taken seats at a table under an arbor. The place had two waiters running across the narrow cobblestone road bringing dishes from a tiny hotel. I walked along the verge, away from the restaurant.

Why had Laval called me with the news of Hamilton Hadad? More than that—come looking for me at the Métropole? Hamilton and I had had no particular reputation for rivalry; I was out of the businesses he ran, had never stooped to dabble in most of them. My friend Jean-Marie Gassion claimed to have heard that Hadad was making war on Mistinguett, but that had been Gardel's subterfuge, disrupting my business before he showed himself and claimed credit. Instead of merely scoffing, I had tried to frighten Jean-Marie by telling him that Hadad was dead. I've never made a habit of lurid fabrication, so Jean-Marie had believed me and accepted the hint that I'd done the job on Hadad. Jean-Marie wouldn't have run to the police with the tale. But if Laval and the frau were squeezing him, he might have tossed them the story. Jean-Marie had never been brave.

Laval would savor the news. So Charles the Arrogant had murdered Hadad! If I went to him now, with my story of Gardel and Paul Chen killing Guiot, Laval would wrap all of us up in the same sausage sack.

I had expected the door to the police to remain open. But it had slammed loudly.

I sat beside Jascha and ordered a coarse country pate and roast rabbit. Drinking sparingly from a pot of Provencal rosé, I enjoyed my lunch. Part of me slipped off with the sparrows that plunged past our little table, over the hillside, and down into a neighboring valley. I'm not given to self-reproach, but I couldn't ignore the facts. Eleven days ago I had had no active enemies but my ennui. Now three hands were turned against me: Gardel's, Guiot's friends', and Laval's. A fine showing for a man trying to make enemies. Ridiculous for a man wanting only to be left alone.

After lunch, I phoned Michael Weeks's home. This time his wife answered, fetched him from the pool. He came on with a tone of surprise. "Charles Mistinguett! Why, how are you sir!" As if we hadn't spoken in years.

I told him I was on my personal phone and the battery was running down.

"Eavesdroppers can intercept anything these days, old horse."

"I've nothing to say that shouldn't be heard. Widely heard."

His tone changed. "You've nothing to say but lies. You should have told me you whacked Hadad."

15

Michael Weeks isn't as strong-minded as a military man. His most fervently held opinions are susceptible to change. Reason, flattery, intimidation: which one will work the change depends on his needs.

"I didn't kill Hadad," I said.

"The police have other information, and it is more convincing than your lies, Charles. Seems you told somebody you'd messed up the corpse."

"I was with Paul Chen when he dumped the body. He had the pieces in the trunk. I told Jean-Marie the body would be hard to identify in order to throw a scare into him."

"The cops won't believe that, Charlie—that you were there innocent like. Not sure I do either."

Now I was demoted to "Charlie."

"Why would I kill Hadad?" I said. "We weren't in the same businesses."

"You've cleaned up your show, Charlie, everybody knows that. No more plonk, no stolen goods. But it still works with Hadad, you see? Hadad looks to settle an old grudge, so you chop off his head. You see? I'm not saying that's how it happened, but the police could like that version as well as the next. It's going to be tough work changing their minds. I'll have to call in favors just to get an audience. It's going to take resources, that's all I'm telling you."

"I suppose it would help if I advanced you some resources."

"I don't like to dip into my own pocket in a case like this, where the client could end up in jail and cut off from his banks. I knew you'd understand."

The client, we both knew, could end up worse than in jail. I said Margaret would wire him an advance.

"It would make my job easier if you came in and explained yourself to the authorities."

And I could sit in jail for eighteen months while the bureaucracy investigated before finally charging, for convenience's sake, the suspect already in its possession.

"The people I talked to made it clear," he said pompously, "that you will receive every courtesy."

I wondered if that nonsense had come directly from Laval, or from a worm in the Justice Ministry, or a maggot at Élysée Palace. Or all three, working together, a thought that made my neck flesh crawl.

"It would be difficult at the moment."

"Where are you?"

"At sea."

"It would help a lot, old horse, if—"

"Go back to your friends at the Ministry and *sell them Gardel and Chen*. That's the best thing you can do for me."

I put the phone away and squinted across the valley, trying to identify the sound that had intruded. It had been there a while, as much as a minute, without really registering. Now I looked and there was a flicker along the treetops. Because of the village's elevation, the helicopter was below me, dipping and jumping like a hornet bothering a flower bed. I walked back among the tables where the view was better.

How far below me was the scene? A mile, I suppose, if you

allow for the twists in the road. A quarter that distance if you fell straight down from my vantage to the road.

A white Lancia emerged from overhanging trees, its shadow creeping forward, and I imagined what the driver was doing, leaning forward and sideways trying to see whatever was hammering the air overhead. As the helicopter dived again, throwing dust across the windshield, the car slowed. Ahead the lane dipped to a crossroads and then descended in long curves to the floor of the valley. I saw what was happening long before the driver understood, because I could see over the hedges that obscured the road intersecting his. A dark van was sitting out of sight, a few yards from the crossroad, waiting its moment. And I understood why it was happening. Some poor fool happened to be driving a Lancia like Margaret's and had been spotted. A half-minute before the prey reached the crossroads, the van pulled out and blocked the intersection. The Lancia stopped. The helicopter hung overhead, whipping up a vortex around both vehicles.

It was too far to identify the men who jumped out of either side of the van. One was taller than you might think and moved decisively. The other was leather-jacketed and totally bald. As the taller man came around the van, I would have bet that the shadow under his nose was a mustache. There was no question, really, General Pourquery. He gestured, and the driver of the car got out. He would have a story to tell when he got home, I thought.

The helicopter had pulled away, and as the vortex settled I saw the Lancia's driver was Hugo. The tall man questioned him for only a few seconds. Hugo pointed up the hillside. The man with the mustache raised a hand, and Hugo crumpled. It was like a magic act except that after Hugo was falling I heard the faint, distant pop.

Beside me Jascha gasped and I realized he had seen most of the drama. The helicopter already was climbing toward our level. We scrambled away from the tables. Martino was crossing the road, working at his fly. As I searched for cover, Jascha said,

"Our guns!" They were tucked out of sight under the seats of the car Hugo had taken.

The leisurely Provencal lunch hours had passed, and not many cars remained along the roadside. Striding past them, Jascha glanced inside an SE, a Peugeot, a Civic. It is not easy these days to steal a better class automobile.

Martino was wandering in the vicinity where Margaret's car had been.

I stood between cars, screening Jascha as he opened the door of the Peugeot. It wasn't worth stealing, a flimsy hatchback 205 with neither power nor size. Its engine had the distinctive buzz of a trapped housefly, and its sound brought two wide-hipped English women in walking shoes and tweed hats brushing between the tables. The nearer one had the expression of someone used to dealing with thieving Mediterranean types. She cried out, "You—little man—that's quite enough!"

Martino wagged a fish knife, turning her challenge to a scream, and swaggered across the cobblestones to join us. I got into the back seat, knees against my chest, and the old man climbed into the front and slammed the door. Jascha backed us out, almost running down the woman. With the knife out of sight, she seemed ready to hang onto a bumper.

The helicopter breasted the hill about then, blowing napkins and tablecloths onto the road. A man leapt six feet to the ground. He was black clad, like a warrior in a Japanese movie, and held a light automatic rifle. He ran between tables, knocking the other Englishwoman aside, and swung the rifle up a moment too late as we swerved behind a stone wall. Between old buildings, the lane was wide enough for one vehicle at a time. If Pourquery's van had arrived at the bottom, we would be blocked. But he had a lot more ground to cover that we did to reach the choke point.

Martino was moaning to himself, not because he knew his grandson's fate but out of humiliation over the boy's desertion. His hand was cupped over his eyes, lifting only when the hammering wheels lost traction and we felt airborne.

"Left or right?"

A hundred feet from the bottom. Jascha needed an answer.

The van would be coming from the right. We were too small to challenge Pourquery's driver.

"Left."

Besides our guns, we had lost files, suitcases and my computer.

We skidded onto the country road, and Jascha jammed the accelerator, trying to gain speed but only making the engine sputter. We couldn't outrun a cyclist, let alone the helicopter. The road snaked between hedges into the valley. A kilometer down, it would join the route on which Hugo had been ambushed.

The helicopter must have stopped to pick up the gunman. Otherwise it would have been right on top of us. Now it swept over the houses behind us and dropped its nose and dived like a hawk. Wind buffeted the car. The aircraft overshot and then hung low above the road a short distance ahead. There was no clearance. We had to stop or slam into the dangling skids. Jascha made a choice and coaxed a little more speed from the car. An instant before we got there, the helicopter jumped out of the way.

The next stretch of road corkscrewed among trees. We were visible from above but inaccessible. I debated stopping. Pourquery would have to deploy his sniper and bring up the van. If we had been armed, it would have been a decent place for a confrontation. The man with the rifle would have made the odds unattractive, but they were going to be that anyway.

Without looking, Jascha said over his shoulder, "Like old times, patron?"

I had never been chased by a helicopter, nor by a man with a rifle, nor by a general. "Shut up. Ahead, turn right."

From the diminished rotor noise, I could tell the airborne pursuit had drifted higher. Where the trees thinned ahead, the pilot would sweep down and try to run us off the road. Or if he had picked up the man with the rifle, he might let him chew us apart from the air. I had no doubt that the rifle would be used if we turned left toward the main route. As soon as we went right, however, there would be communication with the van. What had worked once, driving a quarry to the blind intersection, might work again. Generals are reputed to grow fond of successful tactics. I hoped Pourquery shared that weakness.

I leaned forward and told Jascha, "If you can get us to Margaret's car before Pourquery arrives, you will be able to die with a gun in your hand."

"Life is too kind, Papa."

Pure bravado. His no sillier than mine.

He skidded the car around the corner, corrected a wobble, and accelerated. We had covered three-quarters of the distance to the intersection when I saw that the game was lost. The van hadn't moved far. Ahead, it straddled the road, just behind the Lancia. The only change since my last glimpse of the scene was that Hugo's body had been removed. The bald man in the black jacket stepped away from the vehicles, and Jascha already was standing on the brake and twisting the wheel when our windshield blew. The result was inevitable. The miserable little car rolled onto its side and sped ditchward, spinning like a plate. I knew we had hit the shoulder because gravel burst through the window followed by grassy clods, and then the car turned onto its roof.

I crawled out and spotted Pourquery and the bald one, who fell into crouches and moved behind the Lancia. Jascha crept beside me. His face was bloody but smiling. He said "Uh-oh," because the helicopter was banking to return. I heard a grunt behind me. Martino staggered to his feet, dazed and blinking.

"Get down," I said.

Pourquery fired and Martino clutched his shoulder and collapsed. Neither man on the road advanced. They were waiting, uncertain whether we were armed.

There was a windbreak not twenty meters behind the ditch, protecting a farmer's field. The chances were better that way than here. I told Jascha, "Get going."

"I think I will stay, Papa."

"Your sister needs you, and so does Margaret. And you're no use to me here. You might do some good distracting them, drawing fire." That would appeal to him.

I slipped into the ditch and checked on Martino. He was alive, looking miserable. "Old man," I said, "give me your knife." He passed it left-handed, and I flipped it to Jascha.

The helicopter had turned but was closing slowly, dodging and weaving, expecting us to shoot. The boy waited until the pilot was certain to see him, then scrambled up the back of the ditch and ran for the trees. It is too easy to say my heart went with him. He carried his own. When he was halfway to cover, the helicopter swept wide and low around us, angling to present the sniper with a target. The gunman was a professional, the running boy in every sense an amateur. If the man fired, the rotor noise covered the reports. Jascha may have stumbled, I couldn't be sure, before he disappeared into the wind break.

They came back to take a look at us. There must have been radio communications. It would have been obvious to the marksman that I was unarmed and the old man wasn't a factor. General Pourquery and the bald one stood up and came down the road.

I raised my hands—with little idea of what good it would do—and climbed up to the road, blocking their view of Martino. This was not bravery but resignation. Whatever would happen to me would happen. If Pourquery did not execute me on the spot, the old man might have a chance to crawl away.

His anger demanded immediate satisfaction. He never stopped walking until he had swung a fist into my face. Not wanting a bullet in the back of my head, I stayed on my feet.

"The young man is your son," the general said. "In a minute he will be dead."

When he waved, the helicopter jumped the row of trees and dropped sharply on the other side. It lifted again a moment later, leaving behind a black figure faintly visible between the trunks, who stalked into the field.

"I would enjoy hunting you in the same manner," Pourquery

said. "But the DST commandos and I are pursuing terrorists. . . ." He shrugged.

"Gardel will have a laugh at that."

The helicopter settled in the middle of the road. There were no markings on the fuselage, but the matte black finish would have convinced any passerby that the operation was official. Perhaps it was. Perhaps what was good for Pourquery's reputation was good for France.

He waited patiently, mouth firm, eyes pleased.

I said, "Call off your killer. You don't even have your facts right."

He ignored me.

"'Paul Chen hasn't worked for me for years. The Egyptian muscle never have."

Ignored me.

"They shot Guiot because the three of you weren't paying."

The field behind the trees would be open and flat, good for a rifleman.

"I don't even know what hold Gardel has on you bastards." Had to be more than a pouch full of diamonds. Not even taxi drivers would care.

Indifferent, but not as patient as he pretended. He checked his watch, and the shot came then. It was abrupt, flat, without the lingering echoes of bruised air that come when a gun is fired between hills. This sound burst and died without fanfare. There is dignity in any sound that one assumes has taken a life. I didn't know whether for the shooter the moment was too profound for decoration, or too mundane for memorials. For me it stopped time. My heart crumbled. In those first minutes, there was less normal humanity left in me, I think, than in Gardel.

I didn't throw myself at General Pourquery. He had a gun, as did the bald one who strutted around him like an officious butler. The bald man gestured at Martino, and Pourquery shrugged: let it be for a few minutes, nothing is lost.

"We won't pay," the General said, as if settling a debate. "You have underestimated all of us."

That would be hard to do, underestimating them. The general who wrote of nuclear tactics without ever having known a battlefield. The procurer who arranged a dictator's diamonds for a president. The general who bought soap factories.

"Gardel thought you would pay," I said. "I told him otherwise. Men today have no honor to preserve."

Heavy-handed.

He gave me a tolerant look, and the back of his hand lashed my face. "Now, now."

He was waiting again, not at all patiently. Perhaps the *coup de grace* was customary.

"Marchais, bring in your man."

The bald man lifted a radio and used a click code. He listened but wasn't satisfied. "Report, Loup."

More clicks. More silence.

"Tell him to leave the trophies. We go."

Marchais ordered: "Loup! Leave the ears and the dick for the rats! Get a move!"

Pourquery spoke to me. "Your master . . . Gardel." The name seemed to mean nothing to him. They hadn't gotten that far.

"Paul Chen's master."

He shrugged. "It does not matter."

"It does. Gardel is blackmailing me, or trying to. I had hoped Guiot and I could be allies. He scoffed."

"André frequently scoffed." Pourquery relaxed, deliberately. Our relationship could not become an alliance. He intended to kill me. That he knew for a certainty. And he owed me his own life, for Jascha's. But he wanted to know whatever I knew, so he pretended the situation could be improved. "Who is this Gardel?"

I told him: Spaniard, secret policeman, torturer, murderer.

"What did he use against you?" Pourquery said.

"Old lies . . . and threats against my life. Attacks on people close to me. And you?"

The patrician face turned. He had light hazel eyes. Shrug. "Old lies."

"Gardel fancies himself an enemy of corruption."

"Perhaps he is."

"He doesn't care. He finds patterns in buttons. He was certain he saw a pattern in Guiot, Pourquery, Blasco, and Giscard."

"I will be interested in what he says. If you tell me how to find Gardel—and his men who assassinated André—I will spare this old man's life."

"Send him on his way."

Difficult. Despite being an old fool, Martino had witnessed too much. We were at an impasse, not much sooner than I had expected.

Pourquery scowled. "Marchais! Get your man back to the helicopter."

Marchais lifted his radio again, repeated the clicks, then shouted orders. Pourquery watched the line of trees. A minute passed before the sniper emerged. His rifle was slung over a shoulder. One hand held a radio aloft and shook it angrily.

"Fucking shit," Marchais said.

The sniper trudged to the helicopter. I wondered if the man who wore that hooded uniform knew or cared that today he was executing non-terrorists.

Pourquery flicked a hand at Marchais, and I knew our time had run out. I didn't mind particularly, but felt bad for Martino.

"About Gardel," I said.

"I have very good resources," General Pourquery said, "especially for finding people. There is no need for me to bargain."

He began walking toward the helicopter. Marchais would clean up here. I would try for his throat as the gun turned, for appearance's sake. The radio in the bald man's hand made a shattering noise. He lifted it. I could hear the pilot's complaint. "Colonel—I have been informed I am a hostage."

"What?"

"He demands the prisoners."

Marchais cried, "General!"

The pilot was visible through the reflective glass. The sniper stood in the doorway, attention canted halfway between the pilot and us.

"Colonel!" the pilot cried.

"Shut up!" The bald man aimed his weapon between Martino and me.

"The prisoners!"

I could read it in Marchais's face that he intended to execute Martino for the act's exemplary value. The sniper was too far away to read the man's face. On whatever evidence he could read, the sniper shot Marchais in the hand—heaven knew where he was aiming. Pascal Pourquery threw himself onto the road. Marchais bent to retrieve the gun. I kicked the weapon out of reach before the black-hooded figure could fire again. Enough blood was on the ground. I didn't want him to commit an act he later would regret as unnecessary. For the same reason, as I hustled Martino to the helicopter, I did not tell him that the man lying face down and quivering had shot his grandson.

I looked at Pourquery as we passed.

Finally the General had met armed opponents on a battlefield—and had wet his pants.

When I was near, Jascha removed the sniper's hood. He nodded toward the trees. "Should I go collect the ears and dick?"

"No." I rewarded him for being alive with a hug.

I disabled the aircraft and the van while Jascha bandaged Martino and tied the prisoners at the roadside. Colonel Marchais already had begun his own cleanup at the site. Hugo's body was in the back of the van. I left it and said nothing. I set the General's pistol nearby. If policemen arrived who could not be intimidated, perhaps they would run a ballistics comparison.

As Jascha inspected the Lancia, I knelt beside Pourquery. "Tell Blasco I and my family are not part of this. I don't care what happened in Africa."

His eyes widened. He looked sick with humiliation. I put it down to the state of his trousers. Taking Bokassa's diamonds wouldn't have disturbed the Pourquery conscience. By leaving him alive, I knew I might be signing my own death warrant. I had witnessed him committing murder. I had witnessed commandos of the Directorate for Territorial Surveillance trying to murder civilians. My decision was less a matter of compassion than of pragmatism. A dead security chief from Élysée Palace would have to be avenged—with or without legal niceties. I knew how the DST handles embarrassment. A live general might listen to reason.

"If you wish to rescue your splendid name, Carlos Gardel is the man to see. He has rented the Villa Balzar north of Cannes."

The eyes met mine.

I said, "Next time, no quarter will be given. You would get none now from the old man, if I told him what's in the van. The boy you shot was his grandson."

I glanced down at his trousers, caught Marchais's eye and said, "Every man to his own master."

The drive to Pegomas was uneventful. By dusk I was swimming in Madame Lacoste's elegant pool. By midnight I was awake listening to Margaret telling me I was insane.

16

Madame Lacoste brought me a bottle of cognac and a pot of coffee at ten that evening and offered accommodatingly to slip between the bed sheets. She is close to seventy and wishes she were forty. If she couldn't provide a warm bed, she wanted to provide reminiscences. "I remember your bringing that little sparrow here, Charles. She couldn't have been any good in bed. She wasn't, was she?"

"I don't remember."

"A gentleman would pretend to. I remember her name. It was Mireille. She had the devil in her. You two brought a friend sometimes."

"Edmond?" Her brother.

"No, Yves something. A very little man but so handsome, a jewel. I wasn't certain which of you was in love with him."

"It must have been Mireille."

"Not both of you? I think both. Where did he go?"

She was one of the few people who knew the truth about Yves Bulant, when her memory was working.

"Indochina."

"The sparrow told me, I remember now. You had vowed to kill him if he didn't leave."

"I've vowed a lot of things."

"No doubt. You promised you would always adore Celeste. Even when she grows old, you said."

"That was thirty years ago."

"You didn't seem to mind then that I was a bit more experienced."

"I didn't mind at all."

She smiled, but was happy only for a moment. "Now this mistress you have is twenty years younger than you. That is disgusting, Charles. How absurd to imagine you together."

I poured more coffee, left the brandy alone. She had taken up position on the window seat, which overlooked the pool. The room was on the second floor, with fine morning views of a church tower, behind which were the Alpes-Maritimes rising toward Italy. The villa was obscure, the village barely a name, and I felt reasonably secure and surprisingly content. It had been two years since I had stopped by Villa Lacoste to see how Celeste was getting along. Not even Jascha had known of the old friendship. I was confident that neither Pourquery nor Gardel would find us.

"You should go console the old man," I told Celeste. "He lost a grandson today."

"His heart is broken."

"The grandson used to hit him."

"What a fool then."

"His heart is broken anyway."

"Like you and Mireille."

"Not quite. Not nearly."

The old woman gave me a knowing squint and began nodding. She got off the window seat slowly. I wasn't certain how well she was. Her hands trembled, and her legs were swollen. But she hadn't complained of her usual ailments, hadn't reminded me that she was getting old and I must visit more often if I hoped to find her here. Possibly she no longer believed she was getting old.

"I never thought Mireille was the right woman for you, Charles."

"Who was, Celeste?"

She had too much pride to say herself, because if she had been the right woman then I should have recognized the fact and moved into the villa. There had been a Monsieur Lacoste in those days, but he accepted her habits.

"No woman is right for you, Charles," she said in disgust. "You only humor us. You never confided in me, whatever criminal game you were playing."

"Shall I confide in you now?"

"It's better that I don't know."

"That was how you felt then, too."

"You cannot remember."

I didn't argue. "Go and tend to Martino. Keep him from hanging himself on a door latch."

"The bastard had better not."

"And look in on Jascha."

"He was asleep in a chair, still in his clothes."

Having bad dreams, I knew. The throat of the sniper would become ever more vivid. The blood would become holy water, the flesh sanctified over the years. He was too sensitive not to suffer for the act. And Edith had had to ask whether I was proud.

Celeste took herself away, and I called Margaret again. It was past eight-thirty. Canal 1 had not yet broadcast the first of its many despicable lies. We had spoken barely an hour ago.

"You sound almost relaxed, *mon cher*."

"I am." I'd had long enough to consider the situation to realize it was hopeless. Pourquery couldn't leave mistakes walking and talking—and hinting of whatever it was that frightened him. If Pourquery lacked the will, his former colleague Georges Blasco wouldn't be so weak. A powerful businessman thinks about the world in much the style of a powerful general. Risk was weighed, without the influence of emotion, against reward, and vice versa. We posed an infinite risk alive, none at all dead. Regardless of how long a truce might seem to exist, I would never be able to start a car without expecting an explosion.

We should have been cold-blooded in dealing with Pourquery and his henchmen.

Too late for regrets.

"Are you at sea?" I asked.

"Don't be angry. Ali has had a better idea. We are very safe, very obscure. Safer, he insists, than steaming around the Med."

I wasn't angry. I trusted her judgment, and if she said safe and obscure, they undoubtedly were both.

"Keep in mind," I said, "that we have two sets of enemies. Three if we count the police."

"I will never forget them." She hadn't thought highly of Hugo, but she respected the courage of the old man. She took a lighter tone. "Your daughter has conquered the crew—two of them."

"How many have you conquered?"

"As many as I want. Will you call later? Ali insists on buying me dinner. He is waiting."

I was grateful she hadn't asked what I planned to do. What I had hoped to do was set Pourquery and Gardel at each other's throat. Infections that might cancel one another out. Wishful thinking. It was equally likely they would reach a *modus vivendi* that allowed no room for outsiders.

In the old days I could pack a bag at eleven and be gone by midnight. As long as I had our records and communications, Exports Méditerranée remained portable. It was the staff that had gotten cumbersome. Yet only Jascha, Margaret and Suzy were so close to me that Pourquery might target them if I was out of reach. Edith and Genevieve were vulnerable, but people who wish a man ill seldom harm his ex-wives. Attack on property—the hotel, the negociant, the industrial sites—made no sense. The purpose would be to eliminate Mistinguett, not his well-insured hotel.

But if we fled, where would we go? There was nowhere I wished to live except France. The Mediterranean places that might be open to me—Tunisia, Egypt, not Algeria despite all the slanders, perhaps Malta—were all unappealing in varying degrees. An active man decays in pestholes and goes mad on islands. If General Pourquery was truly determined, moreover, none of those places would be safe. Labor was cheap. Marchais could hire a platoon of killers.

We could join Ali Souidan for an endless cruise. After the first week, I could jump overboard.

If Pourquery was determined. He should have believed me about Guiot, but my innocence had made no difference. He was on an eradication campaign.

We won't pay. Pourquery.

A business arrangement. Of little consequence. Guiot.

Whatever Gardel had on the generals was of more than a little consequence.

All three had been involved: Guiot, Blasco, Pourquery. Possibly Colonel Marchais. Possibly Giscard d'Estaing, but I assumed not; Gardel hadn't tried blackmailing Giscard, or Paul would have told me, couldn't have resisted boasting.

Three generals, thirty years ago.

The diamonds Bokassa had given the French president were old dirt. A scandal in 1981. Diamonds the intermediaries had kept would surprise nobody. Besides which, whose word would there be? Only Gardel's. The sophisticated Frenchman's first response would be a smirk, his second a sigh.

There had to be something more than diamonds: something justifying, even in these days of cheapened life, extortion and murder. Something that would shame a man like Pourquery as much as peeing his pants. Cowardice under fire? Not all three men at once. Treason? That was possible, but how, in Africa? France retains its African empire because no one else wants it. There would be little opportunity to sell out their country in Bokassa land.

As for all the venial sins—I couldn't think of one that would shock a worldly taxi driver. That was my test, wasn't it? Would a taxi driver drop his salami.

I tried a different tack.

A secret is dangerous only while it remains secret. It seemed possible I would be safe the instant Gardel—or *Libération*, the radical newspaper—exposed the generals' secret. I had no contacts among the communist press, but some of my partners might have. If only I had the secret to give them.

Madame Lacoste returned at eleven and dragged me two doors down to her suite, where the television screen showed a photograph of a swarthy and devious face. The man who owned that face was being described by an off-camera voice as an Algerian terrorist.

"The DSGE are familiar with his exploits," a young woman told the camera. "In the early 1980s, it is known he was an assassin—a 'hit' man—for the FLN operating in Algeria. Since then—"

Positively slanderous. My father was Algerian, from the civil servant class, but I spent only my first two months in his homeland. I was raised outside Paris.

"—known to mastermind operations by Algerian terrorists in Europe as well. Today's ambush was directed against a key security adviser to the president, General Pascal Pourquery. The man calling himself Mistinguett was accompanied by several armed assassins, one of whom was killed in a gunfight with the general and a bodyguard."

I admired Pourquery's tactic. He hadn't been able to shut the thing up, so he'd turned it to advantage. If Mistinguett wound up dead at the hands of retired generals, who would object?

"My God," Celeste hissed. "What have you gotten into?" She turned down the sound as the story ended and sat attentively. "I am not worried for myself."

"I understand."

"Before I came for you, they showed a van with all the glass shot out."

"A fabrication."

"And a man was lying dead by the road, beside a machine gun."

"Martino's grandson."

"Dear Hugo?"

"Pourquery shot him in cold blood."

"This is bad."

I agreed.

"You may be shot at any time and no one will ask questions."

I said I knew.

"You must—" She stopped. She had seen too much in life to say anything as fatuous as "set the record straight." Standing up, she shooed me to the door. "I will think on what you must do. At breakfast I will tell you."

In broad terms I knew what I had to do. Throwing myself on the mercy of the generals was futile. Flailing at the French intelligence services would be a comical final gesture. Neither the DST nor its sister, the DGSE, the Directorate General for External Security, could be sued for libel. Least of all by a dead man. My only hope was to deceive Carlos Gardel about my loyalties. I needed to learn what his button collection revealed about the generals. After tonight's broadcast, he would recognize my approach as the act of a desperate man. He might expect a stab at blackmail: my silence about Gardel in return for help of some sort.

I described the situation to Margaret.

"He will pretend to agree, and then kill you."

"He will know I expect exactly that."

"So what? A dead man says 'See! I was right!' You are useless to him, and a liability besides. He has as much reason as Pourquery to see you dead."

"We don't know Pourquery's reason."

"It doesn't matter. There is Hugo's murder—not that anyone would believe you. But if they begin doubting the general on something else, they will doubt him on the murder. He and Gardel both dread exposure."

"I don't think Gardel dreads anything."

"You are mincing words."

"The old man is fearless by his own estimation. What does he have to lose?"

"That makes him even more dangerous. He operates without a normal man's caution. Look at Guiot! Look at Hadad! Paul does those things because he is deranged—he enjoys them. Old Carlos does them because there is no reason not to." She was hurling back at me my own description of the man. "The game cannot have any meaning to him. He knows he will not live long enough to enjoy its fruits. But he has no reason to stop. And he must be extraordinarily vain. *He* is the master. *He* beckons and lesser men come. He encounters an impediment and destroys it. That is how he has always behaved, and who has told the old fool not to?"

"If he hadn't become a torturer, he would have been a great lover. He told me so."

"You see. Vanity."

"But I think you are wrong in saying he dreads being exposed."

"Very well. He 'prefers' not to be exposed, and he will murder all of us to prevent it."

"That's better," I said. "And we 'prefer' not to be murdered."

I told her how I planned to deceive Gardel.

She was horrified. "Charles, you are insane."

I told her why I thought it might work.

She responded. "*And* you are a damned fool."

In the morning, Celeste recommended a scheme much like my own. Ignoring the possible mental infirmity of her age, I felt heartened.

Jascha immediately poked holes. "You won't know whether the generals and Gardel have spoken. They could expose your lie."

"True. But Gardel wouldn't know whether they've told him the truth."

"He will assume you aren't telling it."

Celeste's niece brought another basket of croissants. We were in the yard near the pool, enjoying the strong morning light, slathering the breads with preserves the staff had made from the summer's apricots. The week was expected to be rainy and cold. Suspecting the morning would be the last opportunity, I swam for an hour. It was already turning gray when I came inside and dressed.

I called the hotel where Jean-Marie Gassion was staying at precisely nine-thirty a.m. and made my appointment.

At the overlook, I pulled off the highway. With one of the late M. Lacoste's calabash pipes, a floppy tweed hat and a long slicker, I looked as innocuous as any bourgeois Frenchman having automobile trouble. From the back of Celeste's Renault, I removed the spare tire and tilted it against a fender to improve the scene. While I waited, I unscrewed the car's license tags and concealed them in roadside brush. I was less worried about an observant motor policeman noticing their absence that about someone from Gardel's camp—or Pourquery's—noting the number and tracing the car back to Celeste.

Jean-Marie's rented Mercedes left the highway and drove toward me slowly. He barely glanced at the Renault. He shoved open the passenger door to his car, and I climbed in.

"Where should we go?" he said.

"Wherever you want."

I was curious whether we would be followed. The overlook had two other vehicles parked well away from where I had stopped. The main attraction, a line of misty crags to the north, weren't much to see on a gray morning.

"I'll never forgive you for this, Charles." Jean-Marie's dark eyes were hurt. His round face was indignant.

I didn't answer.

He pulled onto the highway and drove like an old woman expecting to be attacked.

"You are a wanted man—a murderer—a terrorist—and you drag me into it."

I was watching the road behind.

"I should have turned you in."

"You shouldn't have yanked your capital so quickly; I would be better disposed toward you."

"You shit!"

"Look at it this way, Jean-Marie. This will redeem you, in my eyes, square things up. And the tax authorities will never hear a word about you or your money."

We were having the conversation we had had on the telephone.

"I repeat: *You shit!*"

"Steady with the wheel. The little bird who told you about my war with Ham Hadad was working for the man you will call upon. The man's name is Carlos Gardel. Between him and Paul, they have two murders to their credit that I know of. Gardel is an old Spaniard who used to murder people for Franco."

His eyes left the road and he stared at me in horror.

"I will not do it!"

Mention Franco to some people and it's as if there had never been a murderous Communist in Spain. My old friend Jean-Marie had no real politics, but he reacted as the average person reacts who believes he has an alert conscience. Disgust at suitable moments, blank stares at others.

"Of course you will do it. This won't be the first time you've passed yourself off as a movie producer."

Indignant again. "I *am* a producer. You send me, an old friend, to beard an asshole who murders people. He will murder *me!*"

"No," I said calmly. "He will use you to find out how much I know."

"Tell me again," he said.

There was another stopping place a few kilometers into the mountains with another drizzly view of a larch-walled gorge. Jean-Marie sat and smoked a cigar and occasionally whined as I laid out my plan.

He repeated the plan back. I corrected his mistakes.

He sighed. "I tell Gardel as follows. My former friend Mistinguett has phoned me at my hotel. He is shrill and terrified. A conspiracy of generals has branded him a terrorist. But—he tells me—he holds the trump card, and he and I must play it together. One of the generals—Pourquery—was indiscreet. He confessed to Mistinguett the nature of his crime. It was to be a harmless confidence to a dead man. But Mistinguett survived. He now demands I help unmask the generals."

"And?"

"And—of course—I have no idea what Charles is talking about. He hasn't told me what Pourquery confessed. But he's putting the squeeze on me—out and out blackmail. He will squeal to the tax grabbers unless I agree to produce a film exposing the generals. And I don't want any part of it."

"And?"

"And Mistinguett let slip that he was going to wreck things for this man Gardel. I decided if Gardel spoiled Mistinguett's plans it would be good for me."

I interrupted. "At this point, Gardel could shrug off the danger to himself. So you must emphasize that what Mistinguett plans is not an elaborate documentary that will take weeks to produce but a simple video of himself being interviewed, which can be mailed all over Europe and Africa within twenty-four hours. Letting Pourquery's cat out of the bag."

"Yes," Jean-Marie said. "And Gardel will kill me on the spot."

"No, he will want to know if Pourquery actually spilled his secret to me. So he will tell you to go ahead and set up a video recording. He may volunteer to supply a technician. Then once he knows I have the goods—or don't—he will kill us both."

"I knew he would get to that eventually," Jean-Marie said.

I didn't tell him that my estimate depended on Gardel's lack of fear. A rational extortionist, having seen Pourquery's reactions so far, would throw sheets over the Villa Balzar's furniture, bury Jean-Marie in the garden, and vanish.

We drove me back to Celeste's car, and Jean-Marie sped off as I stood in the rain. I inspected the Renault with extreme care. No bomb.

So far, Jean-Marie was working my side of the street.

His call reached me later, in the warmth of Madame Lacoste's kitchen.

"How did it go?" I said.

"Gardel is not as easily fooled as I am. He says the generals protest their innocence even to themselves. Pourquery wouldn't reveal his shame to a man two weeks dead."

A background noise intruded, a dry rustle of a voice.

"So he cares nothing for your video, Charles."

Same sound.

"Your only value to Capitán Gardel is as bait for General Pourquery."

Whispering.

"Because Pourquery and Blasco have made it clear they will not come to terms. So now they are a distraction."

More of the same.

"And to that end *only*, removing a distraction, the recorded indictment of the generals might be useful."

He was still at the Villa Balzar, with Gardel hissing instructions and listening for a sound in my surroundings that he could identify. Jean-Marie knew nothing of Celeste. I wondered how hard a time he'd had convincing the old torturer he didn't know where I was hiding.

I said, "Let me talk to the old man."

Gardel came on. "Gassion will excuse us. He will have a drink, Paul." Feeble voice a bit louder. "A video is a clever idea. Easily adapted, as you see."

"It wasn't what I had in mind."

He muffled a little gasp of pleasure. "Of course not! You underestimated Gardel! We will make the video for television— the hunted terrorist, hiding in the wild, giving his account. Exposing what the guilt-ridden Guiot confessed before his colleagues silenced him. Pourquery and Blasco will have to stop you."

"Why should they be more susceptible to a ruse than you?"

"They have more at risk—vastly more. Their crime would offend even the French. It strikes at the heart of humanity." He fought for breath. "If they were better men, the revelation would drive them to suicide."

I tried to think what disgrace in this day would drive a successful person to take his life. Tried and failed.

The silence stretched for a minute, and Gardel said, "General Blasco, perhaps, would feel too stained to go on. Pourquery— there is nothing he would not try to live down, or deny. When we dangle you in front of him, he will leap, jaws snapping."

And you, I thought, will wait until I'm chewed to pieces, then neutralize Pourquery.

Gardel said, "So—we have an understanding?"

If I said no, Jean-Marie wouldn't leave the villa alive. If I said yes too quickly, Gardel would know I meant no.

"I don't want to be a clay pigeon," I said. "I have to have some protection."

"Of course. These men are not fools. It mustn't appear too easy. It happens I know of a place where a terrorist such as you might go into hiding. It is in the mountains, overlooking a beautiful lake. Paul will take you there. Where are you now?"

"A different lake."

For a moment I thought our alliance was going to founder at the start. I had no intention of risking Celeste. Gardel hated even small acts of defiance.

"I don't believe you understand the situation," he said.

His tone was ineffably smug.

"I do."

"No—" still softly "—or you wouldn't be the least bit difficult. It isn't only your friend Gassion you must worry about. There is a beautiful young woman who arrived here not an hour ago. She is not classically beautiful, I must say, but the flower of youth, you know—even an old man appreciates it. She is most charming, even in a bad temper. She tells me her mother's name is Genevieve."

Suzy.

"Speak to you friends on the boat. Then call me at the villa, and I will tell you what you must do."

17

Keeping Jascha in the dark was essential. He would help no one racing off to storm the Villa Balzar. I put on a cheerful manner around him and Celeste, which he could interpret as Papa's bravado.

Margaret required more delicate tactics. First I had to assure her that as she wasn't Suzy's mother or guardian, she couldn't be blamed for what had happened.

"Nor even a stepmother," she interrupted, tone desolate. "The girl would never accept me as anything but your secretary."

The subject had never arisen between us, the formalities that would confer stepmotherhood on Margaret.

"You couldn't have foreseen how foolish she would be," I said.

We had pieced it together, with the help of a nosy steward on Ali's boat. Sometime in the last twenty-four hours, having conquered everyone on the boat worth her while, my daughter had tired of the game and had telephoned her dago, who rushed down from Bordighera on a scooter. On Port-Cros, the tiny island off which the yacht was anchored, she found a fisherman who took her to the mainland. The steward, who had been jilted that morning, spied on her like a lovelorn puppy as far as Port-Cros. When the fisherman returned, he confirmed the steward's worst fear. The girl who had toyed with his heart had been met by a young man on a Vespa.

A greasy, unhealthy-looking young man with rings on his ears, rivets on his pants, and oil stains on his sleeveless shirt.

"What was his name?" I said Margaret.

"The boy friend? Suzy calls him Puce."

Flea.

"He is the reason Gardel knew so much about us."

"From Suzy?"

"Yes."

Her voice took on an edge. "It is cruel of Gardel to have targeted her. But it is loathsome, if the boy was suborned after they had become friends."

One of these days I would let Jascha ask him.

"I want to join you," she said. "There are things I can do."

"If you arrive without Suzy, Jascha will ask why."

"I will say his sister has run off with a deck hand. You need help, coordination."

What I needed was an army. And a plan. Lacking either, I called Carlos Gardel to receive my orders. He was gracious enough—and boastful enough—to clarify one matter. The flea who had seduced my daughter was his great-grandson. "His name is Narciso," the old man said proudly. "Narciso Xavier."

I kept all the bad news from Jascha as we started north. We passed through the mountain town of Vence before sunup, then joined the N202 highway. The pre-Alpine valleys were filled with orange groves, olive trees, mimosa. As the slopes rose, the cultivation faltered. Across the Var, the peaks rose steep and barren in the early sunlight. It was another twenty minutes before we left the motor route, and ten minutes after that, Jascha found the road to the lodge. It wasn't much more than a graveled track, climbing steeply, then descending in a switchback, and finally disappearing a dozen meters from the building.

Paul Chen and the two Egyptians were already there.

"Wait." I took the car keys, put a restraining hand on Jascha's arm. "Gardel has your sister and there is nothing we can do about it right now. He will be prepared for an attack. We have to wait."

His face darkened. "I knew something was wrong."

"With patience we may set it right."

"With a rifle, patron—"

"Later. Right now, please control your anger."

Jean-Marie arrived ten minutes later in a van decorated with a television station's logo and supporting a small satellite transmitter. Dressed in a brown technician's uniform, the heavily muscled guard I had seen escorting Carlos Gardel emerged on the driver's side. Under Jean-Marie's direction, the guard and Munifal began running cables from the van to the lodge. I followed them inside. Gafar was building a fire in a big stone hearth.

Jean-Marie barely looked in my direction. Paul was bouncing and would have been chatty if I'd encouraged it. Munifal showed me the indifference soldiers reserve for the dead. The bodyguard appraised me covertly. He was to be the executioner. Mistinguett was not meant to remain part of the Gardel equation much past this afternoon.

Gafar warmed his backside before the fire, teasing Jascha with knowing grins and insults in Arabic. The lodge had a half-dozen rooms, with sleeping areas upstairs. There was no furniture, and only the most rudimentary bathroom. I didn't know the lodge's function but supposed a gentleman with rustic tastes might have used it as a hunting camp. There would be boar in the vicinity. The kitchen was in fairly good shape. Paul got the generator behind the main building running. I started a coffee pot on the old stove and used the domestic fussing as cover for scoping out the rest of the property.

The kitchen door opened several steps below the grade. I went out and tried to memorize the dips in the land and the placement of windows and doorways in the nearby outbuilding. If Gardel's plan was to lure Pourquery and company to a rendezvous where they could be murdered, the setting was ideal. But the features that made it well-suited for ambushes — open space, only one outbuilding — made the lodge almost impossible to defend. Anyone under siege would be fighting on at least a three-sided perimeter.

Munifal came around to the rear of the building to urinate.

I went back inside.

Jean-Marie was acting very directorial, waving the arms of his bulky tan windbreaker with its many pockets, stomping in his chafed corduroys, screaming at the bodyguard who was laying cable. As far as I knew, Jean-Marie had nothing to do with the production of television news. I wasn't sure how much of his movie producing I believed. But he was trying to convince someone he knew television. The bodyguard, I supposed. He was afraid the bodyguard would kill him.

"Where did you get the truck?" I said.

"The Chink stole it." He threw me a glance that saved him saying he would never forgive me. "You haven't asked. Your daughter was all right when I left. One of the old man's girls had taken her under a wing. Was trying to sell her on becoming an old man's girl. Short hours, tedious duties. She's fine, Charlie." His grin all but sprayed malice.

"And you — you haven't been injured either, I see."

He blew through his nose. "You can't make me feel guilty that way. You put us both into Gardel's hands. Don't pretend you didn't. Put it here — *here*." The guard had come in the door with a light stand.

"What do you think Gardel has planned?"

"We are going to make a video of a terrorist accusing the officer class. That's what I've been told. Chen has the script."

"Has Gardel let the generals know we're recording?"

"Christ, that would be stupid, wouldn't it?"

"It's what he told me he was going to do. The generals are fighting back, so we will lure them to an ambush."

"Here?"

"I don't know if I believe him. A deal is more likely. The generals pay Gardel, he turns over me and the video recording along with his evidence against them. That ensures the payment is one time. Everybody gets something. Both sides walk away with honor intact."

I didn't quite believe that either. Gardel hadn't gotten to be old by greeting people like himself with his arms spread wide. One hand with a knife would always remain out of sight. If he had made a deal with the generals, regardless of whether he intended to keep it, Gardel would want the video interview completed. It could be a weapon, or merchandise.

I went outside again and tried to see the layout as someone would in planning an ambush. Almost any place could be suitable if the target arrived without defenses. The generals—if they arrived at all—would come prepared for trouble. Given the resources available to Pourquery and Colonel Marchais, they might come better prepared than the ambushers. Looking at the lodge and the outbuilding that way, the setting seemed to be a poor choice. There was no vantage from which a marksman could pick off people in the yard, no natural or manmade feature that offered much advantage absent surprise. The outbuilding was three rooms at most, on a single level, with crumbling walls. The lake that Gardel had mentioned was barely visible through scraggly pine trees a kilometer downhill.

"What are you looking for?" Jean-Marie said.

"How many men were at the villa?"

"I didn't count." His glance took in Paul and the Egyptians, who were being obvious about setting up a security perimeter. "Are they protecting us or holding us?" Jean-Marie said.

"Go ask them. How many men did you see at the villa?"

"A few—I guess five or six besides these clowns. Plus Gardel. Plus the models. I'll tell you, Charles, I would be worried about Suzy. He likes them young."

"So do the rest of us." I thought of Ali Souidan. Ali at least owed me something, which discouraged him from taking samples. I said, "Did you come here direct from the Villa Balzar?"

"Of course."

"How long did the trip take?"

He looked at his watch. "Fifty minutes. Help me with the cameras."

We crossed the yard to the van. There were two shoulder-held, high-definition cameras, also bearing the satellite station's initials. Passing one to me, Jean-Marie whispered. "I hope the little psychopath didn't kill anyone to get this stuff. We'll be ready in a few minutes."

"Stretch it out," I said.

Once we had made an acceptable record, Charles Mistinguett would become superfluous. "Who asks the questions? Or do I just talk?"

"I ask. I think I do. I haven't seen the script."

He handed me a tripod, lifted the other camera, and we walked back to the lodge.

Paul came toward us, saluting. "I'm impressed how you've gone up in the world, boss. The television says you Algerian terrorists whacked a guy in Paris. They showed your picture."

"Jean-Marie says you've got a script. Let me see it."

"No chance. We want spontaneity. Gassion can have it when we get the cameras rolling."

"Pourquery isn't coming, is he?"

"No?"

"If Gardel expected him to come, we wouldn't be making the video."

Paul's face was blank and impassive. "No?"

"You don't blackmail a dead man."

"You know what the Spaniard would say? Maybe the dead man has a family to blackmail. Imagine the kids asking Madame Pourquery, 'What did Papa do in Africa?' What does she tell them? Not the truth. But I'll clue you in. The ambush thing is off.

Wouldn't work. Nobody's spotted Blasco in the field. The old man just wants his movie made."

"Then why the remote location? We could record the interview at Gardel's villa."

"I don't know. What do you think?"

"The gorges are nearby."

Paul smiled at me. "Have you got bodies you want to dump?"

I carried the camera inside and helped set up the scene. Jean-Marie dithered. As a terrorist, should I be sitting comfortably before a fire—or hunched over a bare table with a look of desperation in my eye? Did we want to invest credibility in the recording (he whispered) or, in as much as Gardel might be the only beneficiary, create a transparent record of lies?

"Credibility," I said. "I need to clear my name."

He hissed. "There isn't enough video tape in France for that. Sit over here. Try to look dignified. And sincere. This is not going to be very polished. I will be operating the camera as I recite the questions."

I decided there was no point in delay. Any chance I might have of improving our situation would come after the interview.

I sat in a canvas chair, with the fire partly visible behind me on the left. We decided to dispense with the folding table, behind which the accused could appear to be hiding. I sat patiently while Jean-Marie switched on lights and took readings.

Paul came in the front door and stood behind Jean-Marie during the last preparations. When the camera light came on, only Paul and Gardel's bodyguard remained to watch the interview. Munifal and Gafar were out keeping a perimeter. Jascha had disappeared.

"We'll put an introduction on it afterward," Paul said, handing Jean-Marie a ring-bound folder with a dozen or so pages in it. "Just ask the questions, in order."

"Certainly." Jean-Marie opened the folder, squinted through the camera, glanced sideways. As he glanced at the pages, a frown appeared. He said, "From a professional standpoint, it would be better if I paraphrased a bit, so it doesn't sound so rehearsed."

"Captain Gardel does not want paraphrases."

"It would be much better."

Paul grabbed Jean-Marie's shoulder, spun him around to meet the hand that delivered a loud slap. "What did I say?"

Jean-Marie staggered sideways pulling free of the smaller man. Hand on his reddened cheek, he cried, "You can't hit me, you little Chink!"

Paul was smiling in anticipation. If Jean-Marie struck back, Paul would be able to pull his knife. If Jean-Marie just made a fuss, the knife might come out anyway. The interview could be done regardless of who asked questions from behind the camera. The bodyguard tried to say something to Paul.

I got out of the chair fast. The extra camera was on a tripod ten feet away. I grabbed the legs of the tripod and swung the camera housing against the chimney breast. When Paul whirled at the crash, I raised my hands in a shrug.

"If we're not doing the interview," I said, "we don't need cameras."

He began chuckling, shaking a finger at me, patted Jean-Marie on the shoulder, and took up a position well to the right of the remaining camera.

My interviewer had gotten the message. When we began recording, he read carefully from the prepared text. The first question sounded both stilted and innocuous.

"State your name, please."

I responded. "Charles Mistinguett."

"The answer is not true, I believe." Stilted but no longer innocuous.

Another voice intruded, Paul Chen's. He sounded no less scripted. "It is important to establish your credibility, which requires candor. Your father's name was Boulaida. He was Algerian, a civil servant. All that is true, is it not?"

I settled back into the chair. This little bushwhacking had to be Gardel's handiwork. I decided it didn't matter.

"It is true," I said, "as far as it goes. But it doesn't go very far. My parents were married in a civil ceremony in Delles. As my father was not Catholic, the Church didn't recognize the marriage. When my parents separated and my mother returned to France, she resumed using her family name. That is the name under which I grew up."

Too smooth, I thought.

If they departed from the script, they might have asked if I was a Catholic, and I would have said no. They didn't ask.

Jean-Marie resumed the questioning. He had to improvise around Gardel's script immediately, for questions to flow at all from the preceding answers. With the lights on my face, I couldn't see if Paul was upset.

Q: So there is no one to whom you are known as Charles Boulaida? No terrorist cell operating in France? No underground Islamist group in Algeria?

A: I am known as Charles Mistinguett.

Q: And you are wanted for murder and other terrorist acts.

A: Mistakenly so.

One reason I had been eager to see the script was to learn how it dealt with the question that ought to follow. Did I know who was responsible? It was one thing, and quite permissible, to point to General Pascal Pourquery, Colonel Marchais, and the absent General Blasco. Another to mention who in fact had killed General Guiot . . . though it occurred to me that laying the slaughter on Paul Chen might be acceptable: even to Gardel, the bad habits of an Asian psychopath would eventually outweigh his usefulness.

The script didn't anticipate the brevity of my denial, and Paul had to speak up. "You may want to elaborate on why the manhunt is in error."

"That hardly seems necessary. It is self-evident."

"The police have photographs of you—" Paul's voice choked; he was having trouble sticking to the dispassionate tone they wanted "—photographs of you with the general, André Guiot, minutes before his assassination."

"It is widely known that photographs are easily faked on computers," I replied. "I assume that this was done by the same people who concocted the absurd allegations of terrorism." I stopped myself. They had to *ask* for it.

"Who are these people?" Paul had let himself be led away from Gardel's text. The pages hung limply in Jean-Marie's left hand as he worked the camera controls, no doubt zooming and pulling back every few seconds. His art would be hard on viewers who suffered motion sickness.

"I believe the conspiracy reaches all the way to Élysée Palace," I said. "At the pinnacle is the president's security advisor, General Pascal Pourquery. He has a rather fragrant history, you must know. While in Africa, he helped enrich certain officials of a former government. The scandal is well known. Unfortunately, corruption continues to permeate the political culture of the Republic."

Could I be more pompous? From his silence, I knew it was what Paul wanted.

"Besides Pourquery," I said, "a general named Georges Blasco is involved. And a Colonel Marchais. The late General André Guiot, while not one of my persecutors, participated in the crimes in Africa. He seemed penitent."

I had thought a couple of steps ahead, and clearly Paul Chen had done so as well. He interjected precisely the question I wanted. "Why was Guiot assassinated?"

"Pourquery and Blasco could not rely in his silence. André . . . André Guiot—" deliberate familiarity "—intended to make a clean breast of things."

Not liking to be upstaged, Jean-Marie rustled the script. "Monsieur Mistinguett, what evidence can you offer against these men, who are heroes of the Republic?"

I shrugged. "It is for the public prosecutor to amass evidence. But I am happy to point to the facts. Two days ago, General Pourquery deployed antiterrorism forces of the *Direction por le Surveillance du Territoire* in the area north of Grasse, when absolutely no terrorist events had occurred. Colonel Marchais was present on this operation, during which Pourquery shot to death in cold blood the grandson of one of my employees. It would be interesting to know the pretext Pourquery used to commandeer French government forces—not the nonsense he may have put out since the incident but the reason he provided at its commencement. If the police recovered a body, they might make a ballistics comparison of the bullet inside the young victim with a bullet from General Pourquery's weapon."

I stopped, hesitated, then tried to even the score by adding a plausible lie. "There is a matter the Paris prosecutor might explore—if the public corruption has not reached so deeply as to infect that office." The Paris prosecutor is a Communist who hates the neo-Gaullist in Élysée Palace. Not banking on his integrity, I believed I could count on his animus. "Four days ago, there was a meeting between Pourquery and Guiot in a public park, the Square du Vert-Galant. The meeting occurred at midday. Afterward Pourquery went on foot across Pont Neuf and along Rivoli to the palace. The meeting was a final attempt to dissuade André Guiot from a public confession of what had occurred in the Central African Republic. There are two witnesses, if they have not already been disposed of. General Guiot was accompanied by bodyguards. The prosecutor should have no difficulty learning the bodyguards' identity."

Not my fault if neither bodyguard had survived Guiot's assassination.

There was a hushed consultation between Jean-Marie and Paul, after which Jean-Marie read what I knew must be a closing question:

"Do you know of any additional reason, monsieur, why you have been targeted by these powerful men's lies?"

It was a remarkably clever question. Gardel would know French preoccupations well enough, but he might not have put it into the script had not Guiot been overhead calling me *bicot*.

I fear I answered with more force and sincerity than I intended.

"Of course I know," I said. "They choose me because it is so easy! My father was an Algerian. I am half North African—from the colonies. The generals are mining a convenient vein of racism. I say convenient because in France it lies close to the surface. Closer than we care to admit."

I almost choked on my own sanctimony. But I restrained myself from blurting out the next words on my tongue: "I am not Algerian, I am French!"

As the lights went off and Paul came around the camera, he wore a funny smile. I realized I might have been speaking for him. In France only the totally assimilated are permitted to shed their origins, and then only until it is convenient for some person to remind another, "Oh, he is Russian"—or Czech, or Algerian or *un Juif*—"so what do you expect?" To make amends for their contempt for the lesser races, they open the borders to a flood of ill-suited immigrants who are destroying the culture.

"I think the old pig will be pleased," Paul said.

Jean-Marie backed up the recording, played a few seconds of it in the viewfinder and pronounced the result splendid. "If the police don't shoot you, Charlie, you'll be a spokesman for all the oppressed. Perhaps you will form an organization." His mockery was heavyhanded.

"You are clever," Paul said. "If they ignore you, they are racist."

"That was the idea."

He was nodding, and I wondered what was to come next. On a purely commercial basis, the interview was worth more to Gardel if I was alive to support its allegations.

"Clever," Paul repeated. He spoke to the bodyguard. "Shoot them, outside."

Then he had a laughing fit, waved away the bodyguard. He had trouble getting words out. "Not sure, are you, boss? Have you been too clever or not clever enough?" He composed his face and said, "Munifal would have shot you before the words were half out of my mouth."

He snapped a memory device out of the camera, jerked a thumb at Jean-Marie. "Help load the van. Both of you."

He opened the door, stepped off the porch and scanned the perimeter, checking guards I couldn't see.

Jean-Marie stood near the hearth, hands darting in and out of his jacket pockets. He whispered, "He needs you, Charlie, he doesn't need me."

"True."

His eyes shifted to the back door.

"If you make a run for it," I said, "they'll definitely shoot you."

He thrust his hands into his pockets and left them there, as if finding comfort. Heaven knew what he thought he would do with the damned thing he had slipped into his pocket. Sell it directly to Pourquery, I supposed, or actually have it broadcast.

"And Paul," I said, "will kill you if he discovers you switched memory sticks."

He pretended for all of a second that he didn't know what I was talking about. Then he shushed me, loudly, while watching the doorway in near panic. "For God's sake—"

"You'd better get rid of it while you can. If Paul pops *his* stick into a computer for a look, you're cooked."

When he decided, he moved quickly. He whipped the device from a pocket and dropped it behind the logs burning in the grate. He brushed his palms. "Okay. Let's load the van."

A few drops of rain hit me as I tossed the broken camera into the back of the truck. I pulled on gloves and went over to Celeste's Renault. The doors were still locked. The pine needles I had sprinkled on the hood and trunk lid appeared to be in place. Not conclusive, and in any case if Paul had orders to dispose of us the nearby lake would be quieter than a bomb.

He had called his men from their positions. As they approached the yard, I saw Jascha coming out of the trees zipping his fly. He made a production of how carefree he felt, kicking a pine cone ahead of him. If Paul hadn't been distracted, he would have investigated the display.

Jascha found his way over to me.

"Things are not good, patron." He had picked up the cone

and was bouncing it in his palm. "Six men have taken positions beside the road. They are not Paul's. Two have rifle grenades. Nearer the highway, the road is blocked by several vans."

He waited for a reaction. I gestured impatiently.

"The gunmen are deployed above the ravine. From there the road straightens and rises. We would be driving uphill into their bullets."

I left him and walked back to the lodge. Things were happening much faster than I had expected. I hurried through the kitchen to the back door and studied what I could see of the lake. A boat tied along the shore would have been an unthinkable convenience. There could have been a score of boats turned upside down at secluded spots near the water, but none was visible. A motorless boat, in any case, could leave us on the lake when General Pourquery's rifles came into range. A retreat cross country also was a poor choice. Hiking in the Alpes-Maritimes would be possible in summer, but by now the higher altitudes would have had snow.

I regretted my haste in giving away Gardel's base to Pourquery. I knew Jascha and I had not been followed. The general had set up surveillance at the Villa Balzar, certainly including wiretaps, and had learned where we were meeting and why. The information had come late or his men would have been here waiting.

The van was loaded, and Gardel's bodyguard was in the driver's seat when I waved to Paul Chen. The chop boy was still competent, I hoped.

"Your first instinct," I told him, "is going to be to do a trade. I hope you understand: regardless of what he says, Pourquery won't let any of you live. The road is blocked—riflemen in an ambush and what I would imagine is an assault team waiting in vans."

He wasn't overly surprised. He unslipped a pistol, checked the load. "My first instinct, boss man, is to roll your head down to him, just to see. Then if he still wants to kill me, I deal with it."

"You might regret losing an extra gun."

He gave a disparaging sniff. He called to Munifal to wait and walked with me down to where Jascha was keeping an eye on the scraggly pines that straddled the road. "Your old man says the road is blocked. Is that true?"

"It's true." He described the vans and the riflemen.

"How remarkable they didn't see you."

"If you doubt me, make the drive."

Paul shook his head. "If we make the drive, you will go first." He asked Jascha to describe exactly where the gunmen waited. Then he looked at me, ever the subordinate. "If we all ride in the van, perhaps we can shoot our way out?"

Imagining Pourquery's scoped rifles and grenades, I said, "We would have the comfort of dying together."

Jascha scanned the trees, more worried about moving branches than about the volatile man beside us. He said to me, "I have a suggestion, patron, but I think it will only delay matters. If we don't drive to meet them, they will force the issue. If we block the road, they will have to come on foot—and the area around the lodge is open."

He meant, I gathered, that it was better to be killed by men on foot than by those in an armored van.

"The walls are stone," he went on. "We might—"

"I see the walls," Paul said. He paced. If he doubted Jascha, he wasn't above sending one of the Egyptians ahead and listening for a bang. I worried about how jumpy he was getting. He stopped suddenly and looked up in shock. "I just realized, boss man, you've got no incentive to delay us. If the smelly old fuck decides something's gone wrong, he slits your girl's throat."

He was right. Delay wasn't in my interest. But thanks to Jean-Marie, all I had to trade for Suzy's release was a blank memory device.

"Unless you've got a better idea," I said, "let's get started."

For a moment his round face looked like a Buddha about to throw up. "Drive the van up there," he told Jascha.

The boy shook his head. "We need the van's communications. Papa, we'll have to sacrifice Celeste's car.

Okay? We'll remove the wheels. It will be dead weight. And under the hood—a surprise. We should bring the van and Chen's car near the lodge, blocking the door at five meters—no closer in case they burn."

"Quite the tactician," Paul said. But he went off to circle the wagons, leaving Gardel's bodyguard to ride with Jascha and me in Celeste's Renault up to the road's low crest. No one was waiting. We drove downhill between the close-set trees ten meters and stopped. Anyone coming up the track from the highway would have to push the Renault uphill. Or roll over it. There wasn't room to push it off either side of the track.

Jascha sprang out, flung open the trunk, found a jack and had the left wheels off in two minutes. He rolled them into the brush, while Gardel's bodyguard fumbled the jack onto the right side of the chassis. The man was strong but slow. From the trunk, Jascha pulled a small box, removed the lid and began connecting battery leads through a switch to the gray brick of plastic explosive.

"I thought I told you to throw that into the sea."

He didn't answer.

The last tire bumped down the slope, and our helper kicked free the jack. When he saw Jascha's assembly, he volunteered to return to the lodge.

Jascha popped the hood. Then he was very gentle. He laid the brick on top of the rusted manifold pipe. Rain tapped the sheet metal, then came in an icy rush. Closing the hood three-quarters, Jascha stretched forward and twisted a wire around the latch. He let the hood down with fingertips, pressed it shut.

He nodded to me. Pourquery's rocker switch would detonate the device if the car was tipped or the hood raised.

I started back and found I was walking alone. Jascha had taken several steps and stopped. Rain had flattened his hair. He squinted at the fringe of trees a hundred meters west of the lodge. "Flanking," he said, "at least two."

We hurried down the slope.

Everyone but Jean-Marie was standing near the front door.

Jascha reported, and Paul sent Munifal through the lodge and out the kitchen door carting a rifle. Gafar got deployed in the opposite direction. It was hardly midday, but as the rain hammered down spotting a target at any distance was problematic. We climbed to the second floor, where three dormers faced front. Jean-Marie drifted to a window, and Jascha pulled him away. "Do your watching from the side or they will pick you off," he said.

I went downstairs.

Paul and the bodyguard were making the rounds, window to window.

It was impossible to tell where the shot came from. The sound carried weakly through the rain. It was followed almost immediately by quick pok-pok-poks. Rushing into the main room, Paul crouched beside a west window. There was no sign of the flanking team that had been slipping among the trees. "If that was Munifal," Paul said, with rare formality, "they are fewer."

I couldn't see anything.

"They will withdraw on that side," Paul went on. He saw my skepticism. "The first shot was Munifal's. He never misses. The burst was from one or more survivors firing blindly to cover their retreat." Before he finished there was another dull pop. "Now one more is dead. Good."

Time passed. As I moved from post to post, the visible range shrank to our rock-strewn meadow. I stood near the front door, well to the side, and heard a dull groaning. A heavy engine was straining uphill. I waited in pleasant anticipation. The engine stopped.

The man who came down the road five minutes later was brave, or more afraid of the men behind him than of those in front, at whom he waved a white undershirt as a truce flag. It was remarkable, I thought, Pourquery's confidence in the formalities of war.

The man was medium height and muscular, and at ten meters or so I could see a starkly white face, tightly curled black hair, a heavy jaw.

Paul opened the door. The man came in without breaking stride in the face of three guns. There is a distinctively military kind of courage that regards gunfire as a normal business risk. Most bullets don't wound. Most wounds don't kill.

Tossing the undershirt down with a grimace, the man faced Paul. "The General wishes to offer terms."

"Who are you?"

"Corporal Amat." Back stiff, hands at his sides.

"A corporal?" Paul cried. "We negotiate only with General Pourquery."

"I am to inform you the terms are not negotiable."

I broke in. "What are the terms?"

"You are to surrender Monsieur Mistinguett and the film maker and their equipment. When that has occurred, the rest of you are free to go."

"Safe passage?" Paul asked, wide-eyed.

"That is guaranteed."

"Do you wish them dead or alive?"

The corporal's expression didn't change. "The General has not specified."

His uniform had no identifying patches, nor was there an insignia on his beret. My guess was Pourquery had told the truth and was using DST commandos. Receiving corpses would be a familiar option to a DST corporal.

Paul considered. "What assures our safety?"

"The General is a man of honor."

"Are you sure of that?"

The corporal's back stiffened.

"Probably has good table manners?" Paul said. His tone was confidential, as if he and the corporal shared a joke. Only Paul understood what was funny. The corners of his eyes watched me as he said, "Tell the General we accept."

He pulled open the door, and the corporal marched out. He had gone four steps when Paul shot him in the back.

He slammed the door.

A moment's silence.

Then glass disintegrated in all the windows, and slugs tore up the plaster behind us. Dulled reports followed. I heard a scream and rushed upstairs. Jean-Marie was writhing on the floor, bleeding from the head. Jascha held him down while I picked the larger slivers of glass out of his scalp. "He was too close to the window," Jascha said.

For bandages I retrieved the corporal's undershirt. I tore it into strips while Jean-Marie's fat fingers fluttered above his head. He continued screaming.

Jascha squeezed his shoulder. "I hope you have more dignity than this when they come to kill you."

Jean-Marie's round eyes closed, then opened and the round mouth weakly spewed abuse. "I will," the bloody face vowed to me, "never forgive you."

"Next time, bandage your own head," I said. I tied the last knot, left him and crouched near a window. The other side was not doing much that I could see. A few shadows moved in the distance. Below, the ground wore an icy glaze, and the windshields of the vehicles were turning milky as the rain froze.

The window frame exploded. I ducked back. The other windows' frames had been hit at the same instant. It was impressive shooting. After the first volley had sent us diving under the floor, they had given us time to creep out for a look-see before targeting every window upstairs and down simultaneously.

Paul's voice. "What's the damage?" He meant to us.

"None this time."

"What can you see?"

I crawled over shattered glass, risked a peek. It might have been my imagination, but some of the shots seemed to have come from far on the left.

I bellied over to the stairway. "I think we're being flanked on the east."

He didn't answer. Probably regretted not having taken their deal, whether he'd believed it or not.

Jean-Marie sat up, inspecting his ruined jacket and slacks. He jabbed a finger at me. "If I'm going to die here, Charlie, I want you to know something. I never cared for your first wife, even when I was screwing her."

"Shut up."

A slug hit the wall, and we all cringed.

"All your friends had her, not just Yves. You don't want to hear that, huh?"

"I want to hear something else." In the time it took me to scramble to the east window, a dozen pokety-poks sounded. Various parts of the walls lost their plaster. If Pourquery's marksmen began firing at shallow angles from both sides, the entire front of the lodge could become uninhabitable. If enough lead bounced around inside a stone house, eventually it would find all the soft targets.

For a minute the sleet let up and I heard something behind the gunfire. A kind of rum-rum. Truck engine, straining. They were trying to push aside our roadblock.

When the plastique went off, the concussion shook the building. A balloon of fire shot up behind the road's crest, and scraps of automobile began falling onto the meadow. Jean-Marie looked at me in horror. "Have they brought in a tank?" he said.

"It is possible," Jascha said, tapping the bandage, "that you will die of blood poisoning from the dirty glass."

"You are both animals!"

Jascha joined me at the window. As well-disciplined as the snipers had been, the explosion had thrown them into disarray. Three men in black were running across open ground to reach whatever mess lay out of sight on the road. They were easy targets, but Munifal and Gafar had taken the only rifles.

It was too much to hope that Pourquery or Blasco had been in the van that tried to remove the roadblock. At best we had killed a couple more corporals. The road, however, was now thoroughly blocked. The fire poured up oily smoke, which spread into a low roof over the trees. The generals' little murder spree was turning noisy and messy. Now they would feel pressure to finish quickly. It would be awkward if someone demanded to know whom the DST was trying to kill before the job was done. I couldn't find much comfort in the thought. If the security director of Élysée Palace pointed to the lodge and said "terrorists," what policeman wouldn't want to join in the eradication? To end the siege, all Pourquery needed was a helicopter equipped with rockets. Once darkness fell, he wouldn't need that. His snipers could come close to fire grenades. When it was done, the generals were safe. Nobody would question the elimination of Mistinguett and his cell.

For just a moment, I felt sympathetic to Gardel's complaint. The power and arrogance of the political class bred injustice. Cab drivers shrugged only because of their impotence. Given hope, they would leap aboard any revolution that trundled past the door.

We crept downstairs. Paul was sinking into apathy. Death meant an early rendezvous with the ancestors he had disgraced. His hands were folded, eyes slitted, gaze distant. Preparing excuses. I told him my idea. Faint smile. "Sure, *bicot*."

Jascha cracked the door, very slowly, and I squeezed out on hands and knees, scrambling for the van. Sleet had encased the corporal. That should have warned me. When I reached the television truck and stretched an arm up, the latch was frozen. I curled on my side, pulled off a shoe, and hammered until the ice cracked.

They would wonder about the noise, anyone who had flanked us. If any of them put a scope on the van, I had no cover.

Only a fool has a vehicle's ceiling light come on automatically. Someone who was not a fool had fixed the van's light. I crawled inside and suddenly had reasonable privacy. All the windows were iced. It was dark but I could see my way. I squeezed behind the driver's seat, opened the mesh door and slipped into the rear compartment. I unclamped the camera from its wall mount, collected a loop of power cord. It didn't matter where the cord attached. I tied an end around the passenger's armrest.

Jascha whipped open the door as I reached the lodge. The

movement brought a string of shots that encountered only wood and stone.

"Leave the door open," I said. I had to go back and didn't want a swinging door signaling each move. When the shooting stopped, which was too soon for my taste, I ducked back to the van. The gear selector was in park. I started the engine and returned to the lodge. A half-second later a sniper on the left picked apart the yard between the vehicles and the front door. There wouldn't be any more trips outside.

We set the tripod under an upstairs window, so the camera looked down on the meadow. It took less than a minute for Pourquery's crew to fit the pieces together: running engine, camera feeding to the truck, a satellite feed on the truck roof. He didn't want this operation broadcast on television. A fusillade blew out the van's windows and tore apart the rear panels. Next the upstairs got the attention, but by then we had the camera out of the way. I moved to another window, showed the lens briefly, and retreated with the camera downstairs.

Paul squatted near the dying fire. He nodded approval. "What do you think, boss? Will they rush to finish the job or fall back out of camera range?"

The latter, I hoped, as long as they believed there was any chance we were broadcasting.

"Might buy us a few hours, right?" His voice was flat, as if the outcome didn't concern him. "You figure a general would deploy troops without night vision equipment?"

"No."

He beckoned me closer. "So at most a few hours. Let's do another interview. Set up the camera. The great tactician will point the lens at you. I will ask the questions."

"We need to watch the windows," I objected.

"So the kid will watch them. I will aim the camera. You may as well know why you're going to die."

He got up, slapped the camera, which turned slowly on its tripod. He inserted the memory stick Jean-Marie had given him but needed a minute to figure out the buttons. A battery pack provided power. We had only the room's dim light. He glanced through the lens once. He didn't bother to call for Jean-Marie."Sit down, boss."

I sat.

He laughed. "You should be interviewing me. I dug around in the old madman's files and found out what he's got on these bastards."

My mind was on the windows. "What does he have, Paul?"

"First, remember the diamonds."

Those infernal diamonds again. "Yes."

"Giscard d'Estaing was running France. His buddy the emperor of the Central African Republic, Jean-Bedel Bokassa, knew whose ass to kiss. Giscard jetted down every year for big-game hunting. And now and then, little gifts from the mines. And balling the Empress Catherine. Giscard had that, too. Remember? The burdens of power, eh?"

He waited for me to fill the silence. I said, "I've heard."

"Sure. I told you in Paris. The pimps were three of France's most promising military men. Guiot, Pourquery and Blasco. Two had already made general. The third was on his way. All three were stationed in the Central African Republic. Advising the local army, keeping an eye on French interests. Still with me, boss? They got close to Bokassa. Like minds. He'd served in the French army in Indochina, won the Croix de Guerre and the Legion of Honor. He was a military guy. They were military guys. He was a Francophile. They were French. He had diamonds to throw around. They liked diamonds."

He was interviewing himself. I said nothing.

"How do you think Guiot and Blasco found the capital for their business careers?"

"A commission, I suppose."

"But who would care? Frenchmen expect their big shots to steal. Gardel couldn't squeeze anyone with that. But he had something better. Remember what finally toppled Bokassa?"

I shook my head.

"The locals were pissed at him. He'd spent the country into

ruin. The army was trigger-happy. Then you got students rioting. Hundreds of arrests, lot of kids shot, prisoners never seen again. Then the stories came out. Bokassa was eating the bodies. *Paris Match* even ran a picture of his refrigerator."

That I remembered now. The neo-colonialists at Élysée were embarrassed; the Foreign Legion ousted Jean-Bedel and installed a new puppet.

"He liked to be a good host," Paul Chen said. "Do you understand? Bokassa was a generous host. He invited his friends to dinner at his palace, couple nights a week. Big foreign friends. Guiot, Pourquery and Blasco were regulars all the time the riots were going on. Couple nights a week for a couple months."

The implication was there, but I still didn't get it.

Paul stepped away from the camera. "That's why Pourquery wants us silent. Guiot thought he could live down the humiliation. Bokassa's dead. Where's the proof? One kidney in sauce tastes a lot like another. But it's too much for Pourquery. Be embarrassing, you know, having a cannibal guarding the president."

There was a distant exchange of shots. Jascha came over. "The rain is turning to snow."

I muttered something and got up, mainly to get away from Paul, who was smacking his lips.

"What was that all about?" Jascha said.

"The generals. They don't want anyone knowing what they had for dinner."

"What?"

Surely it had been accidental, I thought. But after the first *ris de*—?

Paul's voice, rising. "Funny, isn't it, the appetites one picks up abroad."

The bodyguard spoke. "They've shot off that transmitter thing. Finally."

We were off the air. Had never been on it. But the pretense was over.

There was a *whump* outside, and the bodyguard reported, "The truck is burning."

I told Jascha, "See if Jean-Marie can travel." I crept over to the bodyguard, who seemed unperturbed by his impending death. "That shooting a minute ago. It sounded like we may have lost one of the Egyptians."

"Probably the east flank. He was never as good as Munifal."

"We can't defend this place from four sides at once."

"I agree. It's a trap."

"If Munifal is still active, we may have a few minutes to get out. Can you convince Paul it's time to run?"

The blunt face turned toward the Chinese. Merciless eyes considered. "He's cuckoo."

"Try to convince him. We need the gun."

I opened the door from the kitchen. The fact that nobody shot me suggested the flanking hadn't yet succeeded. The descent toward the lake was barren for part of the way, a wide open swath hemmed by scraggly mountain conifers on either side. If Gafar was dead, we would be vulnerable on the east flank first. If we bore west, we would pick up the partial cover of the trees and might run into Munifal on the way. We would leave a trail in the ice or snow, whichever we encountered, but that couldn't be helped.

I went back and found Jascha bending Jean-Marie's wrist. "He is too sick to move," Jascha said. "He seems capable of feeling pain, however." He added pressure to the wrist and Jean-Marie screamed.

"Charles! I've done nothing to deserve this."

"You've done more. If you don't get moving, Jascha will stay behind to torture you until Pourquery kills you."

I glanced into the front rooms. No sign of Paul. The bodyguard was at the back door, white-faced and cursing. I looked outside. "Where's Paul?"

He gestured behind us. I heard the car engine start. I ran to the front of the lodge and opened the door as Paul's car fishtailed away from the burned van.

He couldn't get up much speed as the wheels slid on the ice and its skin of snow. The windows were opaque. The driver's door seemed to be partly open. Paul fired ahead as he steered. It was impossible to tell if his shots had any effect. The snow was coming down gently, as if it had all day, and the opposition was somewhere behind it. They had a target, and fired enthusiastically when the car had gotten halfway to the top of the hill. By then he was in range of the rifle grenades. The interior of the car had a small explosion first, and then the fuel tank went and lifted the rear wheels over the roof and the inside blossomed with flames.

I closed the door.

The boat arrived on schedule at three o'clock. Martino held the tiller with a naked foot and aimed a rifle vaguely over our heads. His right arm was bound to his side. He was eager to find someone to shoot. Gardel's bodyguard happily turned over his pistol to me. Pourquery's men were half a kilometer behind us and away to the east. We hadn't come across either Egyptian.

"Have you heard from Margaret?" I asked the old man. I had to reach Gardel before he learned about the disaster of the siege.

Martino shook his head. As Jascha took the rifle, I accepted the tiller. By the time the motor's bray drew the soldiers, we had turned several bends and were out of sight.

18

The retreat entailed a highly circuitous route. Although Martino had brought the Peugeot of Madame Lacoste's niece to the opposite side of the lake, the main roads were thick with Pourquery's forces.

In the pre-Alps, it was autumn again. Still rainy, and coming on evening. Jean-Marie put his head against the back seat cushions and stopped complaining when he fell asleep. The bodyguard pushed the injured man's head off his shoulder and sounded me out on employment.

"You are cool under fire," I replied, "but not particularly loyal."

His broad face registered no offense. "I dispute that," he said.

"No, you are going to be disloyal to Carlos Gardel by telling me what I find if I attack the villa."

Martino leaned across the front seat and pointed a short knife, which he zigzagged in the air. The bodyguard's stare was indifferent. He flicked heavy fingers at the blade, parrying the swipes. I saw the shallow cuts, got the message, and told Martino to stop.

Ignoring his fingers, the guard said: "The young woman is your daughter, yes? Captain Gardel's great-grandson is fond of her, but he is devoted to the old man. Two gunmen from Nice are on the grounds. A third will protect the old man while I am gone. A cook and two other servants are present. Also—two very young women are present who say they are actresses and like the money Gardel gives them."

"How many of them will fight?"

"The great-grandson, Narciso; the gunmen, possibly one servant, and the old man himself."

Five or six, and others who would give the alarm. I couldn't come in shooting. Even if Gardel spared his hostage, the air would be full of random bullets.

When the phone found a signal, I called the hotel. The manager told me regretfully that Aznavourian had not been seen but Laval and other police had taken over the hotel and our conversation undoubtedly was being overheard—at which point they cut him off and I heard Eric Laval's oily invitation to come in and talk. I flipped the phone shut. After a moment I tried Celeste Lacoste. Her niece reported there had been no calls for me. When I couldn't raise Ali Souidan's boat, my unease approached panic. Pourquery and his friends were too accomplished with plastique for me not to imagine the worst.

An injured old man, a whining invalid, and a thug I couldn't trust—the sum of these parts was not a fighting asset. At Vence, I dropped Jascha in the center of the village and drove across a bridge to wait. To fill the time, I phoned the Villa Balzar, handed the phone to Jean-Marie, having told him what to say.

In less than five minutes, Jascha rejoined us, driving an old Escort. He had obtained it from a municipal park, causing no harm to the owner. Our drive out of the mountains has been portrayed by disreputable television broadcasters as a terror spree. Yet another lie. The worst we caused any bystander was inconvenience.

I deployed the others: Gardel's bodyguard slid behind the Escort's steering wheel. Jean-Marie collapsed into the back seat. Martino sat on the passenger's side, needlessly aiming a pistol at the driver. They headed down the N202 toward Nice. I assumed Martino could keep control of the situation without shooting either of his charges. In any case they were out of my hair.

"I hope you have not miscalculated," Jascha said.

I hadn't heard Gardel's voice during Jean-Marie's call, so I had little confidence the old Spaniard had believed my story. The story had combined fact with fabrication. An ambush at the lodge—Jean-Marie cried weakly—had taken the life of Mistinguett. Paul Chen was captured. Only Jean-Marie Gassion and Mistinguett's son had escaped. "In a few hours," Jean-Marie wept, "your own position will be as untenable as Mistinguett's was. The generals will squeeze Chen for information to brand you a terrorist. Once a man has been lied about, killing him becomes easy."

I would have liked to see Gardel's expression as he imagined DST forces at his gate.

"I may tell you," Jean-Marie added, his voice fading dramatically, "no quarter was given to Mistinguett. These generals want no defendants spouting off from the dock. Mistinguett's interview will be devastating enough."

It was a small matter, planting that hook by which Jean-Marie held out hope to a man he had just told there was none. The boy Jascha, he told Gardel, had the recording. Jascha would exchange it for his half-sister at a neutral place.

It was shocking—the ugly thing Pourquery had confessed to Mistinguett. Put one rather off food, didn't it, Jean-Marie lamented with a trembling sigh.

Gardel was planning to escape via the Tende Pass, where the tunnel crosses the frontier into Italy. That is all I can say with confidence—limited confidence, but the inference is logical. The rendezvous Gardel proposed was to be at a layby on the N204, a few kilometers south of the grim mountain town of Tende. The tunnel lies a short drive north of the town.

That was our destination. That was where Jascha stood beside the car at the layby.

The old Basque never arrived.

Neither did a henchman.

I know this much for certain, because I sat on the hillside above the rendezvous, aiming the rifle through the rain at the lighted parking area, until long past dark.

My intention, I insist, was to play fair.

As long as my daughter walked free to the little Peugeot, Captain Carlos Gardel had nothing to fear from me. I had become a little bit like him, doubtful of justice, and thus I was in no hurry to be its instrument. I didn't imagine my personal justice could replace the abstract kind. Often a man must be content with half his spoils, sharing the rest with partners of chance. I was ready to be content with the safety of my children. That is more than fate allows many men.

As far as I have determined, there is not another layby of similar description along that heavily travelled highway. So I cannot offer mistaken venues as an explanation for Gardel's failure to appear. There are other possibilities. Once on the N204, he may well have chosen immediate flight, proceeding directly into Italy on the highway that leads to Turin. It is also possible that the grand manipulator chose to depart France by another means entirely, while his enemies waited by the roadside. Several airfields and ports were within reach. There was not then nor later a general alert issued for Gardel's arrest.

Alternatively, he may have been intercepted by the generals' agents.

I knew only that he had not kept the appointment. An hour after dark, I was close to despair. As I wrapped the gun in its rug and slid down the hillside, my imagination painted lurid scenes of slaughter at the villa. The blame would be entirely mine. Brashly I had given away Gardel's base to Pourquery. A team commanded by Blasco might have been lurking outside the villa even as Gardel prepared to leave.

No prisoners. That would be the code of these disgusting men.

Jascha drove. As we approached the villa, I saw that the gate had been blown open. The twisted left section canted against the stone post like one of those Swiss sculptures. The damp air held the odor of recent gunfire.

Jascha drove full throttle into the courtyard, where he spied a gunman in black clothes and fired several shots at him. The fire was returned, of course. Jascha had never perfected the art of shooting from a moving vehicle. The gunman was too preoccupied diving behind a balustrade to aim properly. No one had been injured when Ali Souidan ran into the lights screaming, "Enough! Enough!" His man emerged from cover cursing.

Ali had taken the villa by storm.

To be precise: he, five members of his ship's crew, and Margaret Aznavourian had done the job. Aznavourian had been the only casualty.

She ran out of the house, saw me and said, "Oh" in the manner of one greeting a late dinner guest. She was flushed, had an endearing smudge on one cheek, and wore a bloody handkerchief around her right forearm. She made a great deal later, in private moments, of the fact I rushed to her spilling endearments without asking after Suzy. A thought that improves my standing with the owner of that precious forearm should not be disputed. Jascha, however, had by then seen his sister through the doorway.

Nonetheless, when I wrapped my arms around the woman and mumbled idiocies about her wound, she scoffed. "It is nothing. A stray shot."

Ali bustled around, clapping me on the back, hugging Margaret, when he had the opportunity, in a way that found her breast, and boasting of the night's heroics.

"Dreadful, Charles! I did not believe we had a chance. It was only after we had detonated the gate and shot our way inside that the kidnappers retreated. Then it was touch and go for a good while until they surrendered."

Margaret smiled. "Don't listen to this fool. Half a dozen shots were fired, none of them well. Your daughter—I'm surprised you haven't asked—is safe."

"What about Gardel?"

She lifted both hands. "We have no idea. When we decided to attack—"

Ali protested. "*You* decided, mademoiselle."

She looked at me. "It was because I assumed you had been killed, patron. There seemed to be nothing left to do."

While I listened to their conflicting versions, Jascha extracted a coherent account from Ali's crew. The defenses had been light—three men who quickly dropped their weapons—and an unarmed cook who reported that Senor Gardel, his great-grandson and a driver had left the villa an hour earlier.

En route where?

Our rendezvous had been in his interest. Even if he planned to leave France, a recorded interview could be used from Spain. When I described the imaginary recording to Margaret the next day, she laughed uproariously. "You place too much value on your own words, *mon cher*. Pourquery and Blasco have little to fear from the rantings of a terrorist. Especially one they have killed. That is what Jean-Marie told Gardel. I think you became too clever. If the old man had known he had an opportunity to kill you, after all the trouble you've caused, then he might have kept your appointment."

"He might have tried to," I said, "and encountered the DST."

"No, they would have blamed his death on you. Your vanity's wounded, Charles, that is all."

She is probably right. What is apparent—and contradicts Margaret's practical view—is that Captain Gardel has not surfaced in France or in Spain. After he left the Villa Balzar that night, the ground might literally have swallowed him up.

Most odd.

We had other things to focus on that night. Ali was chatting up a pretty young woman, inviting her to join him on his yacht. I interrupted the seduction with a suggestion we evacuate the villa. Whether or not General Pourquery had intercepted Gardel, he would get to the villa before the night was over.

"What do I do with the prisoners?"

"Turn them loose as we leave."

"And the women?"

"Make it quick."

I walked away as he tried to recruit companions. Jascha was shaking a finger at his half-sister. I went into the foyer and kissed her.

"Narciso said he wouldn't let anyone hurt me," she said, "and he didn't."

"For which I am grateful." I didn't have time to reflect on all the points on which I wasn't grateful to Narciso.

"I am glad Narciso left before that fat fool Ali showed up shooting. He could have been killed." Her talent for exasperating me was undiminished. "But I miss him already."

"He is easy to miss," I said. I had noticed a good-looking young man from Ali Souidan's crew casting forlorn looks at Suzy. It would have been a shame if the romantic idiot had gotten killed rescuing a prize who was too young and foolish to care for him.

It is detestable, the spectacle created by reporters celebrating the Mistinguett Affair. Where a lie was available, to a man and a woman they chose the lie over the truth. With imbeciles like Eric Laval providing insights into my character to all takers, there were more than enough lies to fill the evening broadcast.

A natural criminal who imagines himself more clever than the police . . . A predator who believes his victims are guilty . . . Behind Charles M. lies only wreckage . . . Because of this shithead, loyal Frenchmen of North African descent find their patriotism questioned.

Loyal Frenchmen! That is the ultimate reversal of day and

night. It is because cells of actual Algerian terrorists were operating in France at the time that the slanders against me had credence. And because of the testimony of two generals whom no discriminating person would invite to dinner. That these two tripe-eaters share tables with so many of the elite speaks eloquently about the state of affairs these days in France.

Much has been made of my failure to offer myself for prosecution. Nor does it sit well with public opinion that Mistinguett and his family have not chosen to make their whereabouts known. I hope a fair-minded person will appreciate my reasons.

I do not really expect justice. Not for myself, even less for Pourquery and Blasco. Captain Gardel's cynicism is, in the strictest sense, appropriate. What is called justice is the punishment inflicted by the strong upon the weak. A man who wishes to survive in this world must be a realist.

Postscript: Michael Weeks, Esq.

It's a deplorable habit of men such as Charles Mistinguett to attempt to mislead whenever possible. They do so even when there is no immediate benefit, seeing deception as like a deposit into a bank account—an asset to be drawn on later. I described the mentality best for the interviewer from *Le Soir*: lies are put away for a rainy day. Acting as such a man's legal adviser is to be avoided, unless one likes him very much, or the pay is excellent. I have found liking this man impossible. He is too busy hiding from me.

I mean that mainly in the metaphorical sense, though for the last month it has also been true literally. I do not know my client's whereabouts. He may be holed up with his "Madame Lacoste" (the name apparently is a pseudonym), but I doubt it. The police have been diligent in their search, and the Mistinguett family would be rather conspicuous. It is more likely they have fled France. This document is his attempt to pave the way to a reconciliation with the authorities.

I am afraid it will do him little good. His lack of candor seeps through the pages like oily fingerprints.

Consider, as a minor example, Charles's scorn for his fellow North Africans. In this document a reader finds a very small sampling. The theme recurs constantly in his conversation. One moment you think you recognize the bigoted Frenchman of the National Front, who believes Europe is being polluted by immigration from the South; the next he confides that his late father was Algerian. "I look it," he says, not seeking to be contradicted. And, of course, he does. He was apparently very fond of his father, yet he denies the emotional attachment that might lead him to strike a blow for Algeria against France. The authorities, understandably skeptical, believe they have their man, or would like to have him.

I was perplexed for a while by his claim, early in this memoir, to have cheated Jean-Marie Gassion in the share redemption, while passing on the advantage to a "complacent" partner. After reflection, I realize this is an example of Charles's intentional disclosures mixing with the unintentional. He expects his narrative to be read by his remaining partners, and he wishes to demonstrate that he treats associates well if they behave as he thinks they should. The unintentional disclosure is that he believes he is entitled to cheat anyone who displeases him. In this case, he clearly views good behavior as silence. It is interesting that none of the partners has come forward, and so far the authorities have found no record of their identities.

Mistinguett is coy when choosing to let us glimpse the truth. Gassion and André Guiot refer to my client in these pages as *pied noir* and, variously, as an "African snake" and "*bicot*." The disclosures mainly serve C.M.'s purpose of portraying these men in a bad light. Timely and selective disclosure is typical of a man accustomed to manipulating the people around him.

That his assistant Margaret Aznavourian stayed aboard for five years speaks obliquely to his redeeming qualities. I accept that such qualities must exist, but cannot point with confidence to any particular one. Mademoiselle Aznavourian could tell us, but on these matters as on others her charm is enhanced by a firm policy of silence. Very few women combine extraordinary beauty with principled loyalty.

As I said, I do not like the man. I am not, despite what he says, an "old friend" but rather an old acquaintance. It is useful to establish this distinction, as it makes me more credible in saying that I believe him to be innocent of the lurid crimes presently charged against him. A mere disposition toward criminality—which C.M. possesses in abundance—doesn't make one guilty of any particular crime. And it is not the bias of a professional pleader that impels me to say a man should be hanged for what he has done, not for what the police *say* he has done.

There is much in Charles's document that taxes a reasonable man's credulity. It is a historical fact, for instance, that Colonel Jean-Bedel Bokassa, who seized power in the largely rural Central African Republic in 1966, was alleged to have eaten the corpses of students who were arrested during civil disturbances. What my client neglects to mention is that the allegations were never proved. Similarly, nobody doubts that France's president, Valery Giscard d'Estaing, received gifts of diamonds from Bokassa (who by the late 1970s had anointed himself emperor as well as president and commander-in-chief), and the stories of Giscard enjoying the favors of Bokassa's queen were widely circulated. But there has been no reputable suggestion that French military officers had much to do with Bokassa's largesse. My client's testament mentions only allegations, supposedly attributed by a dead man (Paul Chen) to a missing man (Carlos Gardel), who is said to have gotten them from Israeli agents working in North Africa. I accept that Charles believes what he says but find the evidence too thin to imagine anyone giving much credence to the notion that French generals practiced cannibalism. The neutral observer, in fact, may see another example of Charles flailing out, assigning vile motives to what was perhaps only a slight overzealousness by the government in pursuing him.

The death of the young man Hugo is another matter. A body

was recovered with a single bullet wound (and evidence of earlier injury) as Charles describes. But no witnesses have come forward supporting a cold-blooded execution. So one is left to believe Mistinguett or believe the DST. To believe Mistinguett requires accepting, among other things, that a young thug would let himself be caught flat-footed and unarmed.

I am not a neutral observer. I am Charles's advocate. But I feel my professional integrity requires that I acknowledge what will be obvious to everyone: my client is not a reliable witness. (Least of all is the shit reliable in his slanders against his lawyer.)

In trying to put the record on an even keel—I couldn't attempt the feat of setting it straight—I also have to address the supposed disappearance of Captain Carlos Gardel, Narciso, and the driver. Here the basic facts are indisputable: The old Spaniard and his companions have not been seen by anyone who cares to say so since leaving the Villa Balzar on the night of October 15. There is no evidence that they took the Tende Tunnel into Italy. There is no evidence they didn't. There is no evidence of a drive across the Cerdagne to the Spanish border, nor of an escape by airplane or boat. There is some conjecture by Charles that Gardel may have run into Pourquery's DST force. This is possible, and if Gardel was setting up a criminal operation in France, it is even plausible that the authorities had an interest in him. Nor would it be unheard of in Europe for a criminal who might embarrass prominent people to be tried *in camera* and dropped into solitary confinement. Thus, there is no compelling reason to disagree with my client's conjecture. And yet . . .

I'm afraid that a less friendly reader, looking at the same facts, will detect the fragments here of a confession. We see Charles luring Gardel from his lair. We see Charles on the hillside with a rifle. We know that his life has been turned upside down by the Spaniard. After all this, conveniently for Charles's claim of innocence, the old man fails to appear.

Personally, I accept Charles's version. But another reader might suspect the rendezvous was in fact kept, at a point farther south, on a less travelled road nonetheless convenient to the area's deep gorges. If the authorities do not have Gardel, Charles may have told them why searching is futile.

To his mind, a law-abiding citizen could do no less.

[Lucille: Don't print this out. I can't call the bastard a shit. See me Monday.]

Photo: Julia Ferguson

About the Author

James L. Ross's novel *Long Pig* was a 2012 Shamus nominee for best paperback original. Reviewing *Death in Budapest, Publishers Weekly* said that "fans of hard-eyed spy novels will hope that this . . . is but the first of many from Ross," citing "twists straight out of a John le Carré novel . . . [and] sardonic wit." Ross's short fiction has appeared in *Alfred Hitchcock's Mystery Magazine*.

2012 Shamus Nominee

Private Eye Writers of America
Best Paperback

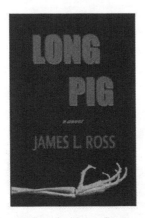

The President's dirty little secret
is worth your life.

Hayes Rutherford did his stint in Vietnam, flying a rescue
chopper that earned him the nickname "Last Chance."
And he was a standup guy forty years later when someone
had to take the fall for a Pentagon billing scandal.

After 18 months in a federal pen, Hayes figures he's done
with the Washington crowd. Working for his daughter
at a Hollywood P.I. firm, his biggest challenge is
keeping the talent sober.

But when rumors ping the White House that somebody
is shopping an ugly movie script about the war-hero President,
Hayes looks like suspect number one. He's about to have his show
cancelled for good, because there are some stories that political
spin doctors can't fix.

LONG PIG   James L. Ross   320 PAGES $15.95 ISBN: 978-1-935797-10-4

"Fans of hard-edge spy novels will hope that this is
but the first of many from Ross. . . .Twists straight out
of a John le Carré novel . . . sardonic wit."

Publishers Weekly

*Patrick McCarry, a down-on-his-luck Wall Streeter, can't get
much sympathy at home. A hedge fund has blown up, and
McCarry looks just the right size for a prison cell. His new
client, knocking around the old East Bloc, talks about building
small engines. But the Balkans are nearby, and what customers
there really want are machine guns.*

DEATH IN BUDAPEST JAMES L. ROSS 180 PAGES TRADE PAPERBACK $9.95

Meet New Orleans private eye Terry Manion

"Cynical and perverse under the skin."
The New York Times on *The Neon Smile*

254 PAGES $12.95 ISBN: 978-1-935797-33-3

254 PAGES $12.95 ISBN: 978-1-935797-34-0

"Dick Lochte is a superb craftsman. . . .
The Neon Smile, with its tantalizing blend
of past and present, is Lochte at his best."
Sue Grafton

"*The Neon Smile* is as colorful and entertaining as
any police thriller ever inspired by the Big Easy."
Joseph Wambaugh

"Chockful of dark humor, wordplay and subtle clues,
the novel is rich enough to reward multiple readings."
Publishers Weekly (Starred Review)

"I couldn't put *The Neon Smile* down. Terry Manion grabbed me
. . . and pulled me deeper and tighter with every passing line!
. . . a helluva good read."
Robert Crais

With new Afterwords by the Author

JUN X 2013

Made in the USA
Lexington, KY
22 June 2013

2/18